Praise for the storytelling of Sharon Buchbinder

Charlotte Redbird, Ghost Coach
"This was a very sweet story about starting over and never giving up by one of my favorite authors."—Linda Tonis, Paranormal Romance Guild

"…when I heard Sharon Buchbinder had a new release, I inhaled it. I connected with Charly right away. The romance between Charly and Dylan is so sweet. The scenes with the cats were pure magic and I loved every minute of it."—N.N. Light Book Reviews

"I laughed at some of the humorous antics of the cats, while the people who make appearances are all unique. *Charlotte Redbird: Ghost Coach* is very original with constantly imaginative scenes."—A. Richard, Amazon Reviewer

Eye of the Eagle
"Sharon Buchbinder seamlessly blends intriguing, sexy characters, and fast-paced suspense in a page-turner you won't be able to put down until the end."—Sharon Saracino, Author, The Earthbound Series

Kiss of the Silver Wolf
"Ms. Buchbinder weaves ancient secrets and modern mysteries into a beautifully written story that will keep you turning the pages."—Roz Lee, USA Today Bestselling Author

Cat's Paw Cove Books

A Witch in Time by Wynter Daniels and Catherine Kean (Book 1)

Her Homerun Hottie by Wynter Daniels (Book 2)

Gambling on the Artist by Wynter Daniels (Book 3)

Meows and Mistletoe: A Cat's Paw Cove Holiday Anthology by 8 guest authors (Book 4)

Hot Magic by Catherine Kean (Book 5)

Reimagining Mr. Right by Wynter Daniels (Book 6)

Familiar Blessings by Candace Colt (Book 7)

Magical Blessings by Candace Colt (Book 8)

Christmas at Moon Mist Manor by Kerry Evelyn (Book 9)

Love Overrules the Lawyer by Kerry Evelyn (Book 10)

Fated Kiss by Darcy Devlon (Book 11)

Charlotte Redbird, Ghost Coach by Sharon Buchbinder (Book 12)

Taken by the Imp by Sharon Buchbinder (Book 13)

The Beachcomber's Buccaneer Bounty by Kerry Evelyn (Book 14)

Romance, Magic, and Cats! 3 Book Set by Wynter Daniels (Book 15)

Charlotte Redbird, Ghost Coach

By
Sharon Buchbinder

Copyright © 2019 by Sharon Buchbinder

All rights reserved. No part of this book may be reproduced in any form or by any electronic or mechanical means, including information storage and retrieval systems—except in the case of brief quotations embodied in critical articles or reviews—without permission in writing from the author.

This book is a work of fiction. All characters, events, scenes, plots and associated elements remain the exclusive copyrighted and/or trademarked property of CPC Publishing, LLC. Any similarity to real persons, living or dead, is purely coincidental and not intended by the author or CPC Publishing.

Published in the United States of America.

ISBN-13: 9798637844272
ASIN: B085MLMNT2

Cover design: Dar Albert, Wicked Smart Designs
Interior graphic: Depositphotos

Welcome to Cat's Paw Cove!

Dear Reader,

Cat's Paw Cove is a fictional, magical town where anything is possible! It was dreamed up by Wynter Daniels and Catherine Kean and is located south of St. Augustine on Florida's Atlantic coast. The name Cat's Paw Cove is derived from the small islands in the harbor, which look like the pads of a cat's paw.

We are so excited to bring you not only our own stories, but also contributions from an incredibly talented group of Guest Authors. With paranormal and mystery romances, historicals, time travels, and more, there's something for everyone.

We hope you'll enjoy reading the series as much as we enjoy writing it. For more information about the Cat's Paw Cove series, please visit:
http://CatsPawCoveRomance.com.

You are also welcome to join our fun, friendly Facebook group where you can interact with the authors, learn about our upcoming book releases and special events, and more:
https://www.facebook.com/groups/CatsPawCove/

Happy reading!

Wynter Daniels and Catherine Kean

Dedication

This book is dedicated with love to my first reader and husband, Dale,
and to our son, Joshua, our daughter-in-law, Elyse, and to our amazing grandchildren, Dexter and Charlotte. They remind me every day that family ties bind with love and priceless memories.

~*~

It is also dedicated to my talented editor, Catherine Kean, who taught this old author many new tricks.

~*~

And to Sharon Saracino,
my funny and fun critique partner and friend. She helps me see the humor in all things in the writing life and other parts of my sometimes crazy world.

Acknowledgments

Anyone who has read my previous novels knows that before I begin to write, I conduct extensive research and steep myself in the materials. This approach enables me to speak through the characters and narrative with rich and correct content. I also rely on subject matter experts and readers from diverse disciplines and cultural backgrounds who provide corrections and feedback to me before I submit a story for consideration for publication.

I would be remiss if I did not thank my readers here, starting with my ever patient husband, Dale Buchbinder, who read every single draft of the story. My deep gratitude goes to the following people for their expertise and feedback: Joshua and Elyse Buchbinder, Toni Chiazza DiBlasi, Deborah Leather, Sharon Saracino, and Susan Willis. Big hugs to my talented and generous editor, Catherine Kean, who shares her knowledge and expertise with kindness.

Charlotte Redbird, Ghost Coach
by Sharon Buchbinder

With the help of hunky real estate agent, Dylan Graham, life coach Charly Redbird and her new kitten have found the perfect home next to a cemetery.

Charly gets a new client right away, who happens to be her neighbor—and a ghost. What could possibly go wrong?

Chapter One

Chicago, Illinois
Present Day

If it If it hadn't been for her uncanny ability to pick winners at the Cicero Racetrack, Charlotte Redbird would have still been working as a prep school lacrosse coach. She hadn't started out playing the ponies. She had a mandatory school function to thank for her winning streak. The high school guidance counselor had convinced the Principal that the teachers and coaches needed to spend "quality time" together, and she'd been ordered to go to the races as part of a mandatory "team building" activity. Once there, it became evident the guidance counselor, an Amazon of a woman, had conjured an excuse to spend time with the good-looking basketball coach—the only marriageable man on staff that she didn't dwarf. Sitting on a hard bleacher in a murk of dust, horse manure, and cheap booze while a statistics teacher droned on about odds and probabilities, Charly squeezed her eyes shut and wished she was home in bed with a good book. If she had had *him* for math in high school, she'd still be in a coma.

Someone rasped in her ear, "That guy don't know squat about playing the ponies."

Twisting in her seat, she spotted an elderly man sitting at an angle from her. His feet swung in the air above the floor like a child in an adult chair. With the brim of his hat pulled low over his face, she couldn't make out his features, just the lit cigarette and the curl of smoke rising to the open sky.

"Were you talking to me?"

He lifted the brim of his hat and glanced from side to side, a wry smile on his wizened face. He removed the glowing smoke from his mouth. "You see anyone else around?"

Indeed, Charly had selected a seat as far away from her so-called colleagues as possible. Infused with alcohol, the prim teachers and stern coaches had morphed into party animals—and it wasn't pretty.

"I see your point." She rattled the racing sheet at him. "I take it you're an expert."

He cackled. "You could say that. What's your name, girlie?"

Mentally rolling her eyes, she responded, "Charlotte, but most people call me Charly."

He tipped his hat. "Nice to meetcha. I'm Billy."

"Well, Billy, if you don't like the math, what do you like?"

He tapped the side of his head. "Horse sense. Look at the fifth race. See that filly named Sally Rivers?"

She nodded. "Says here she's a long shot—a hundred to one odds."

He guffawed. "Doesn't mean she won't win.

She's got spirit. The tried and true ones are fast, but she's feisty." He lit another cigarette and looked her in the eye. "I like the feisty ones."

Was this old guy flirting with her? "Are you aware that cigarettes cause cancer?"

"There ain't nothin' left to eat, drink, or smoke. I might as well be dead." He laughed ending on a hacking cough. "Take my word. Sally Rivers is gonna win."

Charly looked at her watch and groaned. Another hour before the bus would take them back to the school parking lot. *Why not kill some time with a little betting?*

"Okay, Billy. I'm going to put twenty bucks on your filly."

"You're a cheap date, Charly." He raised his thumb up. "Higher."

Payday wasn't until next Friday and she only had fifty bucks on her.

"What if I lose?"

"Mark my words. This is a sure thing."

"What the hell. I'm stuck here anyway. Be right back."

Slapping her remaining cash on the counter of the betting window, she announced, "Fifty on Sally Rivers in the next race."

The clerk paused, shrugged, and handed her the ticket without a word.

The race started before she could leave the lobby, so she watched it on the overhead jumbo screen. Slow out of the gate, the horse looked like she was going to come in dead last.

"Great," she said to no one in particular. "I'll be eating cereal for dinner until next payday." She turned to go back to her seat.

A man screamed in her ear, "Come on Double Trouble, get moving before Sally knocks you into center field!"

It couldn't be. She whirled just in time to see Sally Rivers flying through the crowded pack of horses, bobbing and weaving like a boxer—right up to the finish line. A skirmish of horses came in behind her, no photo finish required.

"Omigod! I won!"

The man beside her threw his tickets down in disgust and stomped away.

With this much money she could pay her rent, have a nice dinner, and still stash some away into savings. Winnings in hand she ran back to her seat to thank Billy.

He was gone, leaving only a whiff of smoke in the air.

A few years and a lot of visits to her buddy Billy later, Charly had a Life Coach Certificate from the expensive and prestigious Traugott Institute for Knowledge of Life. Sitting at her cherry desk, she gazed out the window of her private office in the Chicago Loop and counted her blessings. The blue sky and unseasonably warm weather called her to come out and play, but the new client questionnaire on her computer urged her to stay. Despite her nest egg, she couldn't rely on gambling as a steady income. She loved being self-employed, but she was the toughest boss she'd ever had. Similar to a psychologist in private practice, without clients she'd be out of business in a heartbeat. With a specialty in anger management, Charly received most of her referrals from high school counselors. Others came from college advisors, employers, and on a few occasions, lawyers preparing clients before a court appearance. Her newest client fell into the latter category. He had a habit of breaking things when his temper flared and had been placed on medications to control it. His attorney deemed it critical for him to document his diligence in addressing his behaviors, which included an anger management course. She was so focused on reviewing his candid self-assessment, she nearly jumped out of her skin when a cheery voice broke her concentration.

"Hello! Anyone home?"

She stared at the two women in the open doorway, both blonde and blue-eyed, one older, one younger, and unmistakably related. *Clones.* "I'm sorry, do I know you?"

The older one, presumably the mother, looked familiar. Charly was positive she'd seen her somewhere. *Was she a news anchor for one of the Chicago stations?*

Draped in an expensive silk scarf, opera-length pearls, and a twin sweater set, the attractive woman gave a low throaty laugh. "Of course, you know us. I'm sure you've seen *me* in the social pages. My father, Murray Meadows, was the department store magnate. You know," she made air quotes, "'Meet me under the clock?'"

"Ah, of course, I knew I'd seen you somewhere." Charly rose from her chair and gave a nervous laugh. The department store heiress was frequently in the news for galas benefiting the arts, always dressed in the famous Meadows diamonds and tiara reputedly valued at millions of dollars. There were rumors that the family was so rich, they played board games with *real* money. Maybe she was looking for a life coach for her daughter? It would be nice to have a wealthy client who could refer her to other rich parents. Charly's luck at the racetrack helped pay the bills, but entrée to the Meadows social circle would clinch her career in Chicago.

"What can I do for you?"

"We're your clients," the woman said brightly. "I'm Mrs. Meredith Meadows and this is my daughter, Macy Meadows. You've been coaching Macy for almost a year now. We were in the neighborhood. We thought we'd stop by for Macy's certificate of completion."

Leaning over her desk, Charly ran her fingers across her keyboard and found Macy's file. She pointed to the smiling dark haired, brown-eyed teenager's photo on the computer screen. "There's some mistake. This is the girl I've been coaching for eleven months. She said her name was Macy Meadows, even showed me her school ID card."

Lovely girl. I enjoyed my sessions with her. She'd been very eager to learn. Hoping to go to law school, if I remember correctly. That police report was such a surprise.

The girl smirked. "No, silly, she was my understudy. Get it? She's on a scholarship for ghetto dwellers at my private school, can you imagine?" Her Valley Girl voice ended on an annoyingly high note. "She was more than happy to fill in for me and make a nice chunk of change. Mother paid her two-hundred dollars a session. Overpaid, I think, but *whatever.*"

The same amount of money I charge per session.

Stomach churning, Charly suppressed the urge to lecture the Meadows women about the legal ramifications of misrepresentation. Instead, she took a deep breath and said, "What exactly do you want from me?"

Mrs. Meadows grinned like a great white shark about to devour a hapless swimmer. "A minor detail, a nuisance, really. We just need the coaching certificate to wrap up my daughter's college application. She's already completed her community service. Harvard is holding a spot for her on the Crew team."

A star lacrosse player, Charly had been a student athlete and earned her scholarships to the prestigious university on the shore of Lake Michigan in Evanston before becoming a coach. With legs covered in scars that told a story from every game, Charly knew that teenager had never spent any time in a scull. She locked gazes with Macy. "What position are you?"

Macy giggled. "Twelve, my lucky number." She flopped her arms in an awkward pantomime of rowing. "I love to crew."

And I'm an Olympic swimmer.

Mrs. Meadows' forehead furrowed, and she touched her daughter's arm. "Ms. Redbird, if you would just print that certificate out and put it in an envelope for us, we'll be on our way to the Magnificent Mile for some girl time."

Shameless.

"Mrs. Meadows, I can't provide an anger management certificate for your daughter." Charly pointed at Macy. "She was never here."

"Piffle." The middle-aged woman waved her hand in the air as if to drive off a pesky gnat. "Macy should have *never* been mandated to do this. She was unjustly accused of punching that girl in the face."

"If I recall correctly," Charly said, "The police report said twice in the face, once in the stomach, followed with kicking. The victim sustained three broken ribs."

"Lies!" Macy shouted, her fair skin mottling with rage. "That little witch stole my boyfriend—"

Mrs. Meadows wrapped her bejeweled hand around her daughter's wrist. "Deep breathing, darling, that's all behind you now." She glared at Charly. "Just hand over the certificate we paid for and do it now."

This is getting uglier by the second. De-escalate, but be firm. Do not cave under these unreasonable and unethical demands. Let her know she's not in charge of your practice.

Charly shook her head, "I'm sorry. I can't do that. I would be committing fraud. It's a violation of my ethics and a Life Coach's Code of Conduct. I'd like you to leave my office now."

The mother recoiled with disbelief. "You have no idea what you're doing. If you know what's good for you, you'll hand over that certificate."

Hands clammy, Charly pressed her cell phone to her cheek. "Could you come to my office?"

"Exactly what do you think you're doing?"

A crew-cut security guard the size of a professional football player materialized behind the women and nodded at Charly. "You called?"

"Please escort these ladies out of the building."

He nodded. "This way, ma'am."

Macy whined. "Mommy, don't let her ruin my life!"

Ignoring the uniformed man, nostrils flaring, face reddening, the heiress pointed at Charly and shouted, "I paid for that certificate and you will give it to me. NOW."

Taking a shaky breath, Charly said in a clear, strong voice. "No, ma'am, I will not. Your daughter did not earn it."

Macy's whines turned into wails and foot stomping. "Mommy, *make* her do it!"

"If you don't give it to me, I swear I will have you blackballed at every educational institution in this city—even the ones no one has ever heard of."

The threats only stiffened Charly's resolve. "No means no, Mrs. Meadows." She held up her cell phone. "If you don't go with security, I will call 9-1-1. With your daughter's record and your national reputation, I doubt you want the publicity of being arrested for trespassing, harassment, and assault."

"Mark my words, you impudent little paper-pusher. You will never work in this town again. Hell, hath no fury like a mother scorned." The blonde wheeled on the heel of her thousand-dollar pumps, shoved the guard out of her way, and dragged her sobbing daughter out the door.

Legs wobbling with rage at the audacity of the woman and her threats, Charly fell back into her chair and took deep, shaky breaths. Blackball her at all the high schools in the area? She couldn't do that, could she?

Charly had spent years developing her network of contacts in all the private and public institutions. She'd built a strong reputation. This one disgruntled, lying, parent wouldn't be able to tear that down. She rubbed her arms with trembling hands. Mrs. Meadows was completely in the wrong and she knew it. There was no way she could destroy Charly's hard earned business. No one with half a brain would believe that Blackhawk helicopter parent from hell—would they?

Chapter Two

Cat's Paw Cove, Florida
Early December, Present Day

Grandma Redbird had told her that every resident had a cat, or two, but that advance notice hadn't prepared her for the sight of the large Victorian mansion's wraparound porch. The railing was festooned with green garlands accented with red and gold—and cats. Lounging cats, stretching cats, standing cats, strolling cats, rolling cats, rubbing cats—cats, cats, cats! Rocking chairs meant for humans seated two and three felines, in furry piles, paws splayed in all directions. An elderly woman rocked with a cat on her lap and another one wrapped around her neck. All bicolor, the herd of kitties sported stripes, spots, or random patterns in an endless variation of shapes. Two huge cats sat like Egyptian statues at the top of the bannister, black tails dangling down in question marks, masked golden eyes boring a hole into her forehead.

Unnerved by the intensity of the feline gazes,

Charly wondered if she had time to jump into Pearl, her white hybrid, and drive back to the Palmetto Motel before her grandmother spotted her. As she turned to open the driver's door, an unmistakable voice called to her.

"Charlotte, I'm so glad you're here." Leaning on a cane, her round-faced grandmother with her signature short salt and pepper hair waved from the doorway of the Feline Fine Retirement Home. "Grab your suitcase, honey, and come on in."

Feeling guilty for even thinking of running away, Charly followed her grandmother's directions and yanked her rolling bag out of the packed hatchback. All her worldly belongings stuffed into one compact car. Grateful she'd never bought, only rented furniture in Chicago, Charly gave herself a mental pat on the back for saving those moving costs. Still, her life in one little car made her feel—small. Forcing herself to put some cheer in her voice, she called back, "Be right there, Grandma."

As she climbed the stairs, the masked cats' heads turned like owls, marking her every move. She nodded hello to the elderly woman covered in kitties and avoided paws, and tails.

Grabbing her into a bear hug, her tiny but strong grandmother crushed the air out of her lungs. "So happy to see you, my little one."

Resting her chin on top of the older woman's head and speaking in a squeak, Charly said. "I could go to a motel, you know."

Grandma gave her an extra hard squeeze, then released her. "Not on my watch. As long as I have a roof over my head, my home is your home. Come on, let me show you the place."

Chattering like a tour guide, the older woman pointed out the spacious sitting rooms, the community dining room, the recreation room, the front desk bookended with a Hanukkah menorah and a Kwanzaa candleholder, and the administrators' office suite behind Christmas wreathed doors. She lowered her voice. "The administrators are all from the British Isles. We're allowed to have guests stay over weekends. We don't have to tell the fat cats you'll be here past Sunday. They'll never even notice."

How did her grandmother figure a five-foot-eight, auburn haired twenty-seven year old would blend in with the gray-haired octogenarian crowd? She kept her doubts to herself. It didn't matter. She wouldn't stay long.

They entered an elevator and Grandma Redbird pressed the button for the second floor. "I should have moved in here sooner. It's good to be with people like me."

The elevator stopped and she led Charly to a door decorated with scarlet cardinals. "The administrators think I don't know what they're doing with this. In case I forget to read, apparently, they figured I'd remember my name with the red birds." She chuckled and turned the key in the door. "At ninety years of age, I've forgotten a lot of things, but I have *yet* to forget my name. Come on in."

It was like walking into Charly's childhood home, only smaller. Grandma Redbird had decorated her small apartment with photographs of the family and her extensive shell collection. Her prize possession for as long as Charly could recall was a large conch, with an odd pattern that almost looked like a face. Tightly wrapped, it was particularly unusual because it had no opening, just a seam where the original inhabitant would have put its foot out to inch along. The conch sat in the center of a coffee table in a small sitting area with a couch, chair and television. A modern galley kitchen with a table for two led to a closed door, she assumed was a pantry. Through an open door, Charly could see a queen-sized bed. A brown and white spotted cat stood, stretched on the couch, and greeted them with a chirp.

"This is Cowry." She rubbed his head and sat on the couch then patted the cushion next to her. "Have a seat. He won't hurt you. He's a good boy. His sister, Junonia, on the other hand, is a bit of a sneak. She looks like him, but she has a brown mask. Enough about me and my cats. What about you? What happened? I thought you were doing well in Chicago."

Charly sighed. *What a fiasco her life had been since May.* She didn't want to tell her grandmother what a failure she was—but she'd never been able to keep a secret from her. Tears welled up in Charly's eyes. "I don't even know where to begin."

Her warm brown eyes gazed into Charly's, a traction beam for truth. "Was it a man?"

She barked a little laugh. "I wish. No. It was a well-heeled woman. A billionaire." She told her grandmother about the incident with Meredith Meadows. "I didn't believe she'd follow through on her threat. You know, I'm a small fish and she's this big shark. But apparently, by saying no to her, I'd chummed the waters. She said she was going to get me. And she did."

Grandma Redbird patted her hand. "Go on."

"She's so used to ordering people around, she probably had someone do it for her. The outcome was the same. I was blackballed at every school in the Chicago area. She lodged a complaint with the Chicago Better Business Bureau, said I'd violated my contract. I sent a rebuttal, but the complaint stays on BBB's website for three years. Thanks to her, my college, employer, and legal referrals dried up. She even tried to get my Traugott Institute for Knowledge of Life coaching certificate taken away—at least she wasn't successful at that. Traugott's widow called me and asked me what happened. She commended me for being ethical and for standing my ground, said her dearly departed husband would have been proud of me."

"You've hit a bad patch."

"You've got that right." Her shoulder hitched with sobs. "I tried to think where I could go where no one would know me, so I could start over. It's the holidays—I just wanted go home."

"You were right to come here. What with your parents selling the house in Tampa and moving to the Cotswalds, well, that wouldn't work. It's an enormous fifty-five plus community that's like a theme park for seniors." She waved her hand in the air. "Not a good fit for you. Besides, you'd never meet a man your own age."

Charly snorted through her tears. "I'm not in the market for a boyfriend, Grandma. Right now, I'm trying to pull my life out of the trash heap."

"What about Miami? You could live with your big brother."

"The last thing Brendan needs while he's studying to become a nurse anesthetist is for me to drop into his life with all my baggage. I couldn't do that to him. He needs to focus. Besides, I'm already working with a real estate agent here in Cat's Paw Cove. Maybe you've heard of him? Dylan Graham, goes by the name of Big D?"

"Oh, he helped my friend sell her home. Said he's a wizard at finding the perfect forever home for people."

"That's a funny way of putting it, but yeah, that's what I'm hoping for. A permanent place to hang my hat—and my coaching certificate."

"Now you're talking." Grandma pointed at the kitchen counter. "There's Junonia." A masked cat stared at Charly. "She's checking you out."

"Are all the masked cats like that? The two jumbos on the porch looked at me like they were TSA Agents checking me out for bombs."

Grandma Redbird chuckled. "A lot of the cats in Cat's Paw Cove are related to the Sherwood cats. You'll have to ask Big D to take you to the Sherwood House. Quite a story. Anyway, they say all the Sherwood cats are charmed, but the ones with masks are magical. Although I confess, the only magical thing I've seen about Junonia is her ability to disappear for hours then reappear under my nose. But, I think that's just a cat thing." She waggled a finger at the cat in question. "Right, Princess J?"

Junonia sniffed and turned her back to them.

"I get the feeling she thinks we're peasants," Charly noted. "Here to serve her tuna and milk on command."

Grandma Redbird gave a sly smile. "You wouldn't be wrong. Let's go down to the dining room so I can introduce you to my friends. After dinner, I've got DME Bingo."

"What kind of Bingo?"

"We all bring a piece of durable medical equipment to spice things up. Whoever gets the winningest Bingo cards is allowed to choose their prize. It's always interesting to see what people bring."

"Isn't that gambling?"

The older woman shook her head. "No money involved—just our little contributions."

Charly reflected on her time at the horse races. After that first trip, she'd gone every week—and had bet on Billy's picks. She had taken care not to attract too much attention with her wins, tossing in some losers to keep a low profile. Over time, the other customers at the racetrack had begun to acknowledge her and say hello. Before she left Chicago, she had gone to the track one more time to say thanks and bid him a farewell. She had trolled the bleachers and bar, asking the regulars if they'd seen him.

"Billy. I'm sure you've seen him around." She had repeated the same thing a dozen times. Short old guy, wears a newsboy cap, smokes like a chimney, raspy voice, talks like he's from Brooklyn?"

At last, an old timer had lifted his head off the bar. "Billy? Billy Guillermo the jockey?"

A jockey? Why didn't I think of that? It all makes sense now. "Have you seen him?"

Grinning a nearly toothless smile, the elderly man had said, "Honey, the last time I saw Billy was at his funeral."

Her heart had stuttered in her chest. What an ungrateful person she'd been. She'd taken so much from him and had given little in return, except maybe a few laughs. The cigarettes must have killed him. "He's dead?"

The man had nodded. "Very."

"What happened?"

"He lived by the horse and died by the horse, right here at this racetrack, twenty years ago."

The jumbo screen had gone in and out of focus, and the room had twirled around her. She had grabbed a chair to steady herself.

Raising his glass, the man had said, "To Billy. May his spirit be with us at the Cicero Racetrack—forever."

She shook her head, pulling herself back into the present and her grandmother's apartment. The shock of being forced out of business and out of Chicago must have rattled her brain. No way that man she'd spent hours laughing and joking with had been a ghost. They must have been pulling a prank on her. Ghosts were only for Halloween, spooky stories, and haunted houses—right?

"Charly? Where'd you go?" Grandma waved a hand in front of her face. "You okay?"

"I'm sorry I spaced out. Did you say it was dinner time?" Her stomach growled. "The last time I ate was in Georgia."

"Goodness, why didn't you say something sooner? Let's get down to the dining room." Grandma Redbird stood, using the cane to steady her as she rose. "We have a nice menu with lots of choices, plus we can order some wine with our dinner—albeit by the thimbleful."

"Quick question—where am I sleeping?"

"That couch opens up into a sleeper. Don't worry. I'll have it made up."

"You have maid service?"

Her eyes twinkled. "Doesn't everyone?" She grabbed Charly's arm. "Let's go down so I can introduce you to my friends. I bet a few of them have grandsons that are eligible bachelors."

"Grandma!" The last thing she wanted was for her doting grandmother to parade her in front of the residents announcing her availability.

"Oh, hold on. I need to grab something for Bingo later this evening." She moved faster than Charly expected and came out of the bedroom, holding a black item aloft. "Back brace. Very sought after. Let's go."

A year ago, had someone told Charly that she'd be looking forward to a meal in a retirement home, she would have been doubled over in laughter. *Never say never.* She caught a glimpse of herself in a mirror on the way out. Puffy-eyes, chapped lips, hair falling out of her ponytail, the one thing she was grateful for was that most of the residents were too old to even see her well. No one else her age would be in the room. She sighed. *I can be myself.*

The dining room buzzed with conversations and laughter. Grandma introduced her to a table of four gray-haired women in assorted shapes and sizes, all wearing large flowered print dresses. "The Flower Girls," Grandma whispered as they left earshot. "They don't own any clothes without floral patterns."

Another table of women, one with long bright red hair, was intent on a game of cards. "The Players, very serious about their games. They eat and play at the same time."

A table in the center of the room held three Asian women and a balding Asian man working at a jigsaw puzzle. "The Puzzlers. Keeps the brain fit. They finish a puzzle a day and like to speak in riddles."

A long table beneath a large window bore an

assortment of holiday decorations in miniature, along with a doll's house. When she drew closer, Charly realized it was a made to scale model of the retirement home. A group of women fussed around the decorations and the tiny Victorian model, placing wee decorations with precision. "The Decorators. I dare not interrupt them. They need to focus. This is a busy time of year for them."

A loud table in the corner greeted them with a big shout of hellos. "The Debaters. They can argue over the best kind of bread, peanut butter, or orange juice. You name a topic; they'll give you a debate."

The rotund man with a bad toupee proffered a bright white grin. "Would you like an argument?"

"Not today, Frank, but thanks." Her grandmother urged her along. "We could be here all night arguing with him." She pointed her cane at a table in a cozy corner of the dining room. "Here's our table, dear. Darla, this is my granddaughter, Charly."

Like a deer in the headlights, Charly froze in place. An attractive seventy-something blonde woman clung to the arm of a large man who looked just a tad older than herself—twenty-nine or thirty years old.

He looked up at her with dark, mischievous eyes, and smiled. The dimples made a flock of butterflies take off in her stomach—that plus the fact he was movie-star handsome. He looked as surprised as she felt. Face flushed with embarrassment, the idea that homeless people looked better than she did kept looping through her mind. When he spoke, she knew the rumbling tenor that sent shivers down to her toes. She'd spent hours on the phone with him discussing houses, listings, and prices.

Smile broadening, he rose, towering over her

and extended his large hand. "Big D. Delighted to meet you."

Chapter Three

Dylan grasped her small hand in his and gave a gentle squeeze, short enough to be polite and long enough to validate what his psychic dowsing rod had pointed to during their phone calls. This woman was powerful—and she didn't know it. Beneath that power, a wave of sadness rose and fell like the tide. People moved to Cat's Paw Cove for all kinds of reasons, some magical, some mundane. Her motive flashed into his mind with a stab of shame and pain: failure.

"I am so delighted to meet you," he said. Delight was such a milquetoast word. He wanted to say ecstatic—but knew alarm bells would go off in the beautiful auburn-haired woman's head. Reaching into the pocket of his blazer, he extracted a handkerchief and extended it to her. "Once you get used to the pollens down here, your allergies will subside."

Surprised registered on her face. "Thank you," Charly accepted the soft cloth and the lie. "They're killing me."

Grandma Redbird piped up. "If we don't sit

down, they won't serve us."

Charly rolled her eyes. "Okay, Grandma." They obeyed the command.

Dylan said, "I know you've reviewed all the listings I sent to you. We are low on inventory in Cat's Paw Cove. There is talk of building some condos and apartments in the area, but that's in the planning stages."

Grandma Redbird tapped Dylan with a menu. "We're here to eat, young man, not talk business. My granddaughter is starving."

Head down, a rosy glow creeping up her neck and cheeks, Charly ran her finger down the menu. "How's the grouper?"

"The food is so good; I'd swear it's made by elves." She chortled. "But we all know *they* only exist in fairy tales."

Darla stared at Dylan and raised her eyebrows.

Charly has no idea she's in a retirement home for magical beings.

He shook his head, and Darla's eyes widened.

In fact, FFRH was a hotbed of mythical creatures—wood nymphs, gods, goddesses and spirits of gambling, Chinese dragons, genies, trolls, medicine men and women, witches and wizards, and, yes, even brownies. Looking for better opportunities than churning butter, sweeping floors, and washing dishes, the brownies had immigrated to America from the British Isles. They cooked and cleaned, and they were the FFRH administrators, attending to all details of managing this magical home.

"Mrs. Redbird," Dylan asked, "What do you recommend?"

"Big D, call me Grandma Redbird. Everyone

else does. You can't go wrong with the chicken. Melts in your mouth. Plus, the mashed potatoes and green beans are delicious. Just wait 'til you taste the cornbread. You won't be able to stop eating it."

She waved a uniformed teenager over to the table. "We're ready."

Dylan ordered the chicken and Charly said, "Make that two, please. The cornbread sounds heavenly."

"Three." Darla handed the server her menu.

"Four—and bring us a bottle of Chardonnay. And real wine glasses, not those thimbles you usually bring out." Grandma looked around the table. "What? I'm almost a century old. You think a little wine is going to kill me?"

Laughing, Dylan agreed. "I think once you hit eighty, you have the right to eat and drink whatever you want—as long as no one gets hurt."

"Thank you." She turned to her granddaughter. "What are you doing sitting between Darla and me? You need to get closer to Big D. He has a house for you."

"Trying to get rid of me?" Charly changed chairs. "Sorry," she whispered to him. "I don't recall my grandmother being this bossy before."

"I hear the older we get, the more we become like ourselves." A whiff of a perfume he couldn't place wafted toward him. Floral, with a hint of vanilla. Something a wood nymph might wear. Puzzled, he slid his hand across the table to reach for his glass of water, "accidentally" bumping hers. *No. Not a wood nymph.* He'd never sensed this type of magic before. *What the heck is she?* "Let's set the house talk aside for now. How was your trip?"

"Exhausting. I wanted to get as much distance between Chicago and me as I could. I put the pedal to the metal in Pearl, my little hybrid. It's a wonder she didn't give up halfway here."

"Why the rush?" Failure beat its nasty little drum, a pulsing throb like a headache. "Escaping someone?"

She sighed. "You could say that."

He didn't push. When she was ready, she'd tell him the details.

"We all have someone like that in our life. A bad boss, a rotten ex, or a crappy job. Sometimes bad people or situations push us along in our lives, to become a bigger person, or to utilize all our abilities. Ready or not, here you go. Life is funny like that. We have to look back to see what our turning points were. Maybe this is one for you."

Charly sipped her sweet tea. "Easy for you to say. Looks like you've been a success all your life."

"Ah, no." He shook his head. Even with his ability to spot psychics—what he called his dowsing rod—he didn't feel successful—which in his mind meant magical. He was more like a talent scout who could spot supernatural beings but didn't own any particular ability. "I used to sell cars, got paid on commission. I was terrible. My boss told me I needed to go in for the kill."

"Sounds predatory."

"It was. I couldn't sell people cars they couldn't afford. Even if they could afford one, my boss wanted me to upsell. You know—hey, you need undercoating, and don't you want those windows tinted? I steered customers to used or inexpensive vehicles and told them they didn't need the extras. The customers appreciated it, but my boss didn't. He fired me."

"Where were you when I bought Pearl?" She pointed a chicken leg in the direction of the street. "I'm positive I bought all those add-ons. Probably added a couple thousand to the price."

"At least you're not a family of four on poverty level income." He recalled the Latino couple working two jobs each just to make ends meet. The day he sent them to a reputable used car dealer was his last day on the job. Face twisted with rage, the owner of the dealership had dressed him down in the middle of the blacktopped parking lot as the sun blazed overhead, glinting off hundreds of windshields. Shards of rage had slammed into his torso and head, leaving Dylan with a migraine that lasted a week. At the time, however, all he could say was, "Thanks." He had removed his nametag, handed it to his puzzled supervisor, and had driven home. A week later, he woke up feeling human and decided he would never sell anything to anyone who couldn't afford it. Unlike his former boss, he was not a landshark.

She nodded. "You're right. I have a good-sized nest egg to invest in a house. And I can move in immediately. I don't have a stick of furniture, so that's an issue."

"How would you feel about a well-maintained, sweet little bungalow that comes completely furnished—with housewares? Turnkey condition. Pots, pans, dishes. The only thing you need to buy is a mattress for the queen sized bed."

Her eyes lit up, then a skeptical expression replaced her initial look of joy. "Sounds too good to be true. If inventory is low, why is it still on the market? Is it built on a swamp? Or an Indian burial ground?"

"Well…." She was good, really good. Whatever her talent was. "Not exactly."

She took a sip of wine, her hazel eyes boring into him, waiting for a response.

"It's at the end of Bent Tail Boulevard, near the train depot."

"Is that it? The trains are noisy? *Pfft*. Come on. I lived in Chicago near the L—the elevated train system—and slept with the windows open."

"And…it's across the street from—"

"Dessert?"

Saved by the server.

"We have apple pie, pecan pie, key lime pie—"

"He'll take the key lime pie," Grandma Redbird called. "In fact, we'll all have that."

Charly raised her eyebrows. "You were saying?"

"Sherwood Cemetery."

She laughed so hard; all the surrounding diners paused their conversations to see what was so funny. "Is. That. All?" She chortled the words out between gasps of breath. "I thought you were going to say it was next to a landfill or a toxic dump. Jeez. You had me going there."

"You don't care?" This was unexpected. Most people ran the other way when he said the neighbors were quiet because they were dead. "Really?"

"Can we go see it?"

"Now?"

"After you have dessert," Grandma interjected, "you are free to do whatever you want. But you *must* eat the pie."

Dylan and Charly exchanged glances and burst

out laughing.

When he found out who was responsible for Charly moving to Cat's Paw Cove, he was going to send that person a large bag of Florida oranges and a hand-written thank you note.

Dylan parked in front of the butter-colored stucco house with the sea green awnings and shutters and waited for Charly to park her white hatchback. The windows of her car revealed boxes packed so tightly, he wondered how she'd get the stuff out of the car without yanking it all out at once. She parked and tossed a glance at the palm tree-studded Sherwood Cemetery as she climbed out of the driver's seat.

"The neighbors seem nice. Quiet, too." She smiled. "Thank God for the train depot nearby, or I'd have trouble sleeping."

"I'm glad you have a sense of humor about the location. A lot of other people didn't."

"I like the outside," she said, stepping through the doorway into a small sitting area. "It looks like a little gingerbread house with the scalloped edging under the roof."

"I'll give you a moment to look around. It's not huge, only 750 square feet, but you'll probably spend a lot of time outside on the screened-in lanai." He lifted a flyer off the table and read the specs to her while she walked around. "One full bath with clawfoot tub and shower, updated galley kitchen, sitting area slash living room, bedroom with queen bed and dressers, plus a closet. Firepit on the lanai. What you see is what you get. Fully furnished."

She opened a cabinet door in the kitchen. "Goodness, I haven't seen this china pattern since I was a child. Vintage Franciscan Rose—and it looks like a complete set. That's amazing. Look at this—I'm sure I've seen this cobalt blue crystal somewhere before."

"If you buy the house, it's all yours. You can sell them at Black Cat Antiquities in town. Lucian's a great guy. He'll give you an honest assessment."

"Sell it? Heck, no. I love vintage things. You should see my wardrobe. I frequented all the consignment shops in Chicago. You'd be amazed at what you can find in those stores. I think I might have been born in the wrong era. The forties were definitely my time."

"This house was built in the forties, right after World War II."

"Then it's meant to be." She nodded. "Yes. I'll take it."

Dylan's heart staggered. "Don't kid with me like that. You didn't even ask the price."

She pointed at the paper in his hand. "It's right there. One-hundred-ninety-five-thousand." She tilted her head and squinted. "How much are the taxes? I can't read it from here."

"Thirty-five hundred a year. But you could file an appeal to get it reduced." This was the first time he'd ever sold a house in less than an hour. He didn't want her to feel pressured or worse yet, cheated. "How about you just give me a check, earnest money. Then you can have it inspected. It's an old house. No one's been living here for a while. Things can break, even if they're not used."

Charly folded her arms across her chest. "Is the owner going to pay for the repairs?"

He shook his head. "She passed away three years ago at Feline Fine Retirement Home. She was a beloved resident." He didn't add she was non-magical, but they loved her anyway. "Her children live in Michigan. They're selling it as is, want to get whatever they can."

"That explains the price. Three years?" She whistled. "It's immaculate. Not a speck of dust. Who's been cleaning it?"

"A local service. Very reliable. Excellent work." The brownies at FFRH had a subsidiary cleaning company that took care of this house and many others in Cat's Paw Cove. He held back that bit of information. "I can give you their contact information—if you're serious about buying the house."

"I fell in love with this place the minute I walked in the door. It's like it's been waiting for me." She smiled and ran her hand along the frame of the kitchen door. "I believe houses know the right owner for them. This little place spoke to me, made me feel welcome." She glanced at him. "You think I'm silly, don't you?"

"Not at all. In fact, I think you're amazing." *She's going to fit into Cat's Paw Cove just fine. If she ever discovers her own powers.* He led her out and turned the key in the lock. "Let's wait until tomorrow to start the paperwork. I don't want you to feel rushed."

"Are you kidding? Where's your office? I'll follow you there. I don't want to wait one minute longer than necessary to move into this adorable cottage." Charly stopped walking. "Did the former owner name it?"

"Not that I'm aware of." *She named her car. Why not the house?*

"Good. I'm going to name her something that goes with my new town. Hmm. Tail's End? Redbird's Cattage?" She snapped her fingers and grinned "I've got it! Furever Home!"

"Really, so soon with the puns?"

"Are you kitten me? I'm just getting started."

Dylan put his palm over his face and moaned. He really liked Charly. He hoped he didn't screw it up the way he did with the last woman he cared for.

Chapter Four

Driving back to her grandmother's place, Charly smiled, happy for the first time in months. The house was cute, and Big D was even cuter. Dare she hope for a decent relationship in her new town? The high school where she had been a lacrosse coach had been slim pickings for dates. Her clients had been, for the most part, teenagers, college students, and angry men she wouldn't date in a million years. And the only guy she really liked at the racetrack had been a ghost. *Ack.*

No. Billy was not a ghost. That old guy at the bar had been three—no—four sheets to the wind. Had he been tested; he probably would have blown a blood alcohol level triple legal limits. An unreliable narrator, at best, a wet-brained confabulator at worst. Billy must have died that week, and the drunk confused the past with the present. Nope. Not a ghost, no ma'am, no how. End of discussion.

A little voice piped up in her head. *Still....*

Heading back to FFRH, she belted out a pop song at the top of her lungs to shut that voice up.

"Because I'm happy—what the heck?

Holiday decorations had sprouted from the roof to the lawn of the retirement home. Charly didn't know where to look first. Up top, Santa's sleigh and reindeer looked as if they had just dropped in from the North Pole. Red legs with black boots wriggled in a faux chimney. Icicle lights dripped from the eaves, and an electric candle burned in every window. A family of snow people waved from the right, and an army of nutcrackers marched to the left of the candy cane-lined walkway.

She climbed the stairs to the front door to the tune of a 1940s version of a holiday classic,—*J-I-N-G-L-E BELLS*—and stopped at the top of the stairs and whispered to the guard cat on the right, "How did you let this happen on your watch?"

He narrowed his eyes and hissed.

She put her hand up. "Nuff said."

A ten-foot tall blue spruce, its top bent under the ceiling, engulfed the lobby. Boxes of decorations stood open nearby, a glinting collection of all colors of the rainbow, plus strings of bubble lights.

Bubble lights? Do they still make those?

Residents stood in clusters, the same groups that had been together at dinner.

The Flower Girls wrung their hands weeping and chanting in a strange tongue.

The Debaters barked at the Decorators. "What, you couldn't get a taller tree?" "Have you heard of this new thing called a tape measure?" "Were the Douglas firs all gone, or do you just like the color blue?"

The Puzzlers riddled everyone. "What's fifteen feet tall, blue, and too tall for this ceiling?" "What do you call a Decorator on a bad day?" "What's on all fours in the morning, two in the afternoon, three in the evening, and one at night?"

The Players were placing a wager on how fast the tree would fall over. "I'm betting twenty minutes, tops." "Are you kidding? That thing is jammed into the ceiling. I'm betting twelve hours before the tip snaps." "You're both wrong, I bet you the Administrators will be out here in less than ten minutes to fix this mess."

The Decorators fussed at one another. "This is all your fault. That dollhouse is to scale. Didn't I tell you the tree you put in was too big?" "It is *not* to scale. It's off by one quarter of an inch. I told you this wouldn't work." "I said to use a Fraser fir, but no one would listen to me."

A tiny woman dressed in a matching brown skirt and top with her name—Agnes—sewn on the blouse pocket, stood on the desk, and shouted in a British accent, "STOP TALKING!"

A blanket of silence fell on the bickering bunch.

"This is unacceptable behavior." Agnes' bun quivered on the top of her head. "Everyone has bad days. The Decorators have been working very hard to get us in the Christmas spirit—and look at you. This is *not* what St. Nick is expecting of us." Her green-eyed gaze roamed over the crowd and fell on Charly. The little woman pointed. "Who is *that*?"

Grandma Redbird materialized at her side. "My granddaughter, Charly. Come to visit me for a bit."

"You know the rules about guests, Mrs. Redbird," Agnes said in a clipped tone of voice. "One weekend, that is all. This is not a youth hostel."

Voice dripping with honey, Grandma

responded, "She'll be no trouble at all, I promise."

"I'm standing right here." Charly put her arm protectively around her tiny grandmother. "I'm not a stray cat. There's no reason to be mean. I won't be here for more than two days. Maybe less. I just put an offer on a house on Bent Tail Boulevard."

The little woman's expression changed from anger to disbelief. Her voice fell to a stage whisper. "Which house?"

"The only one for sale on the street—the little bungalow with green awnings across the street from the cemetery."

"Mrs. Redbird, you need to talk some sense into your granddaughter. Surely there's another place available for her? A condo or apartment? That house is—"

"Perfect." Charly retorted. "I've even named it. Furever Home."

Agnes' eyes rolled back in her head, and she fell off the desk in a dead faint.

Once the hubbub died down and they were back in her grandmother's apartment, Charly said, "What was that all about? Talk about feeling unwanted."

"Don't take it personally. Agnes has a habit of poking her nose in other people's business—and getting worked up so much she faints. She's a drama queen."

"She needs to get a new wardrobe. That brown

outfit did not suit her at all. Looked like something a cookie-selling kid would wear."

"Perhaps you could offer her some fashion advice," her grandmother said with a sly grin.

"I suspect it would fall on deaf ears. Hey, would you like to see the house tomorrow? It's adorable."

"I'd love to see it. Speaking of adorable, what do you think of Dylan?"

Not even in town one day and her grandmother was arranging dates like she'd arranged Charly's play dates as a child.

"You trying to be a matchmaker, Grandma?"

"Well, I did sense a little spark at dinner. You *were* having a good time."

Heat flushed her face. "Big D is funny—and seems like a nice guy. But he's a salesman. It's his job to be charming."

"Valid point, my dear." She patted Charly's arm. "Your bed is all made up. You look like you could use a good night's rest."

Yawning, Charly agreed. "Is there a second bathroom?"

"No, dear, but you can use mine. I'll be out of your hair in a moment. It's Bingo night."

"I forgot about that. Have a good time. Don't lose your back brace."

"*Pfft.* I have plenty of them," Grandma gave her a peck on the cheek. "Sweet dreams, my darling Charly." Her grandmother stepped lightly for an old gal with a cane and waved at Charly as she closed the door saying, "You're my favorite girl."

She hoped Big D would have some good news for her tomorrow. Agnes had made it clear the *unwelcome* mat would be put out for her if she tried to overstay. After a long, hot shower, she turned down the blankets on the pull-out couch. Yawning, her gaze snagged on the conch shell. *Had it gotten bigger?* She shook her head. *Don't be ridiculous. Shells can't grow.* She fell into bed and immediately began to dream.

The entire cast of characters from earlier that evening milled around. The guard cats sat on the desk in the lobby, their tails swishing. Her grandmother was angry—so bizarre. She'd never seen Grandma raise her voice, much less shake a fist at someone. What was she saying?

"Agnes, how dare you single out my granddaughter and give her a hard time? One more word out of your mouth about her and you know what I'll do to you?"

"I'm sorry, Tatesta, it was insane. Everyone was overwrought—and I spotted a regular person in our midst."

"She's not a regular."

"She's not magical, Tatesta. Not a speck of it coming off her."

"She's young," her grandmother's lips thinned. *"Furthermore, a regular lived here for years. Why did you allow her to stay if you dislike them so much."*

"She was under the protection of the Players. I can't intervene in the affairs of gods and goddesses. You know that."

"But you're happy to mess with my family?" She shook her cane at the little woman. "Not another word. Do you understand?"

Charly jerked out of sleep. *That was weird.* Her grandmother's name wasn't Tatesta. *Where did that come from?* A line of light shone beneath her grandmother's bedroom door, and a high-pitched female voice said, "If I have to eat one more can of tuna, I'm going to scream. Why not a little variety? Salmon, halibut, even chicken would be a nice change of pace."

Was the TV on?

A lower male voice said, "Sister, I agree with you one-hundred percent. I do love me some hamburger. Medium rare, ya know, not well done. Bleh. Why even eat meat that burnt?"

She tapped on the door. "Grandma? Is it okay to use your bathroom?"

Silence.

Did she fall asleep with the TV on? She pushed the door open. The television screen was black, the bed still made up. Only the two cats were in the room, the male licking the female's ear. They paused, stared at her with their golden eyes, and returned to their grooming.

Shaking her head, Charly used the bathroom, pulled the bedroom door behind her, and fell into bed. She hadn't had dreams that odd since she was a kid and had the flu. *Crap*. Was she getting sick? One more thing to add to her to-do list: find a doctor.

Just as she was dozing off, her grandmother came in. Charly called out in a voice thick with sleep. "Win anything?"

"No, dear." The cane thumped across the floor.

"Better luck next time, Grandma."

"Only if the Players let me win."

"Mm-kay, night."

"Sweet dreams." She whispered, "You're not regular. Not regular at all."

Chapter Five

A few days, several rounds of faxing, and two-hundred-thousand dollars later, Dylan signed the final document and handed Charly the keys to her new bungalow. He felt guilty that he hadn't broken a sweat on this cash deal. Emails and express couriers' deliveries had expedited the closing, along with a clean title and zero liens on the property. Not a single hiccup—and most real estate deals had *some* hitches. It was almost as if the previous owner had been under the guardianship by someone—or something—and had transferred that protection to Charly. He shook his head. *Don't be ridiculous.* The only ones he knew with that kind of power were the gods, goddesses, and spirits of gambling at FFRH. This beautiful woman with the innocent, freckled face couldn't be a player—could she?

"This has been the easiest sale I've ever had in my life. Can I help you get settled in? It's the least I can do."

"No, I'm good." She pointed at the car.

"Everything I own is right there. Not much to unpack."

"Dinner's on me, then. Pie in the Sky makes great pizza."

"It's a deal." She flashed a dazzling smile. "Let's say five?"

Even when her eyes had been puffy from crying, she'd been pretty. Today, she'd dressed up for the closing, wearing an emerald sundress that brought out the flecks of green in her hazel eyes. Standing on the sidewalk outside his office, he admired how the Florida sun glinted through her auburn hair, transforming her into a heart-stopping, ethereal beauty. Boy, he hoped he didn't screw this one up.

"Perfect. Do you drink wine? Whiskers and Tails Winery has a great chardonnay."

She cocked her head and frowned. "Are you planning to get me drunk?"

He stammered, "N-n-no."

"Just kidding," she laughed. "I love chardonnay. See you later. I can't wait to get to Furever Home."

After plugging in the Christmas lights, he placed the CLOSED, PLEASE CALL ME sign on the door, and locked up his one-person storefront. He wanted to go by Coquina Castle and pick up some brochures for his office—and to take one to Charly to see if she'd like to go there with him. It was a fascinating place. To this day, no one knew how that jilted lover had moved all those huge rocks by himself into those arrangements. Maybe he hadn't been human. Always a possibility in Cat's Paw Cove.

Envy spiked through him. If only he were magical, then maybe he'd feel like less of an outsider.

Three years ago, he had moved to Cat's Paw Cove to get over a bad break-up. Connecticut had nothing but sad memories for him now. His psychic dowsing rod had been part of the demise of that relationship.

Things had been a bit rough. She had been anxious about a job she'd applied for. His grandmother's health was failing. The last straw, his ex-girlfriend had said, was when he cried because she was crying. That evening they'd met at their favorite Thai restaurant in downtown Hartford. She had arrived in tears.

He had put his arm around her shoulders and eased her into a seat. "What's wrong?"

Shoulders hitching with sobs, she said, "They passed me over for the promotion I wanted. For the last five years, I've practically lived at that company. Who did they give the job to? The CEO's *nephew*, a slacker. Now that jerk is going to be my boss, in the job I should have had, earning the pay I should be making." She had cried harder. "I loved my job. Now I hate the idea of going in to work."

Tears had welled up in his eyes. "Oh, honey, I'm so sorry. That's not fair." He pulled a handkerchief out of his pocket and handed to her.

"Thank you." She looked up. "Why are *you* crying?"

"I can't help it," he shrugged. "It's the way I'm wired."

"Men don't cry." Her eyes narrowed. "You're making fun of me."

"No. I've always been like this. I can't explain it."

Still teary-eyed, her face had twisted with rage. "One of the worst days in my life, and this is what you do? You mock me?" Gathering her coat and bag, she stood, nearly knocking the chair over. "If I wanted a mood stone, I'd buy one. Don't ever call me again."

One month later, his grandmother had died, leaving a modest trust fund to his younger brother and an ugly old wooden chest to Dylan. Made from white oak, the impenetrable box bore crude carvings of his grandmother's initials, K.H. *Katharine Harris.* It would have been nice if she had left him instructions on how to open the case. Instead she left him a cryptic note.

My darling Dylan—

I'm sure you are wondering why I left your brother a trust fund and gave you an old box. Please take good care of it, as it has great worth, although it appears to be of no value. Even though people will turn away in disgust, keep this in a safe place. When time is right, all will be revealed to you. Meanwhile, do not envy your younger brother. He does not have your talents. I suspect his life will be less interesting than yours.

Remember, I will love you forever.

Grandmama

Despite wondering if his sharp-as-a-tack grandmother had become dotty as death approached, he honored her wishes and kept the container in a safe in his bedroom closet. Nestled beneath his pile of legal documents, the box had not once called attention to itself in any manner. No moans in the middle of the night, no sudden explosions. It sat there waiting for—what? He shook his head. *Talents?* Other than being able to spot a magical person by shaking hands, his only gift was mirroring other people's emotions. At this point, his extreme empathy was more a liability than an asset. What did Grandmama know that she hadn't shared with him? His grandmother had told him she'd led an interesting life before setting down in

Willimantic as a stay-at-home wife and mother of two boys. One son had died in Vietnam, the other, Dylan's father, had gone to college and become an accountant. Her adventures, whatever they were, had gone with her to the grave.

Seeing the sand colored castle up ahead, he picked up his pace. Only a few more hours to get ready for his dinner date with Charly. He couldn't wait.

As if standing by the window, Charly opened the door at the first ring of the bell. "I see you've got your hands full, let me help you."

"Take the pizza and the African violet. I've got the rest under control." Giddy with excitement—was she feeling it, too?—Dylan lifted the wicker basket with care.

"Where can I set this down?"

She pointed to the coffee table decorated with a large conch shell. "That works." She placed the cardboard box in the oven. "Two hundred degrees should keep it warm until we're ready to eat."

A tiny meow came from the basket.

Shoot. He'd wanted to surprise her. So much for that.

She tilted her head. "What's that? Do you have a cat in there?"

"Maybe." He grinned. "Maybe not."

Another meow.

Charly reached for the lid of the basket at the same time he did—and their hands collided. The jolt to his nerves was like a smack to his funny bone, except this didn't stay in his elbow. The shock radiated up his arm, kicked him in the chest and threw him on the floor. Looking up at Charly, he tried to catch his breath.

"Omigod," she cried, "Are you okay?" She knelt beside him. "I was a lacrosse coach. Took care of lots of injuries on the field. Let me check you—"

He put his hand up. "I'm not sure that's a good idea."

"Why not?"

"It could happen again." He didn't like it the first time. He sure as heck wouldn't enjoy that feeling a second time.

"Don't be silly. It was just a discharge of static electricity. Your shoes rubbing on the carpet must have done it. You stumbled back and fell. That's all."

That was not static electricity.

She reached for him. "Let me take a look at you, please? I have lots of ice."

With great trepidation, he prepared to be shocked again.

An intense expression on her face, Charly examined his fingers.

Nothing. No shocks. Not even a tiny zap. He did not imagine it. Whatever it was.

Her hands ran over his shoulders and back, then his legs.

"Any pain?"

"No." Just the agony of falling on his butt in front of the woman he wanted to impress.

"Think you can stand?" She rose and offered her hand.

He waved her away. "I'm okay. Embarrassed,

but not hurt. Way to make an impression."

More meows emerged from the wicker basket, and it began to shake.

Charly pointed. "May I?"

He laughed. "The cat's out of the bag, so to speak."

She lifted the wooden lid and squealed. "They are so *cute*. Look at those widdle paws and the cute pink noses. And the spots! Oh, look one has a mask, like the cats at my grandmother's place." She looked up at him, her eyes sparkling, pleasure radiating from her like an aura. "Where did you get them?"

"Coquina Castle. Someone left a basket lined with a red and green blanket and filled with kittens. No sign of their mother. Other people took some, too. I took a boy and a girl. By the way, unless the cats drank it, there should be a nice bottle of chardonnay in there, too." He shook his head. "So much for making a grand entrance."

"Memorable, that's for sure," she said with a chuckle. "Which kitten do you want?"

"I've been told you need to have kittens in pairs—otherwise they get lonely and have no one to play with—except you. They may look innocent, but those tiny nails and teeth can shred fingers and toes."

She picked one up and waved its paw at him. "He yikes you. Wants you to do home with you."

"I'm never home. Seriously, you should keep them both."

She handed him the boy. "Okay, here's an idea. I keep them both here, and you have to promise to visit them as often as you can. Okay?"

The kitten clung to his shirt with razor-sharp claws. "It's a deal."

"What do you want to bet they'll be litter trained in a week?" She rocked the girl kitty and wiggled her ears. "Look at the mask on this girl. And this spot here," she pointed to the kitten's side, "looks like a target, doesn't it?"

He stroked the boy's back and his little motor began to run. "What shall we name them?"

"Hmm." She buried her nose in the girl's belly. "How about Pizza Pie for the boy and Little Pie for the girl?"

"Ha. I like it." He handed her Pizza Pie. "I stopped and picked up some pet supplies at the store. They're out in the car, I'll go get them."

"You thought of everything." Charly continued making baby noises and talking to both kittens.

Despite his ungainly arrival, it seemed his housewarming gifts were a hit. *Thank goodness she likes cats.*

As he came up the walkway with the bags of food, dishes, litter, litter pans, and toys, Charly looked past him.

"I guess someone's visiting the cemetery. Seems a little late in the evening, doesn't it?"

He turned and scanned the horizon. "I don't see anything but palm trees and tombstones."

"Right there." She pointed at a cluster of shrubs. "See? That woman in the dark dress. I think she's looking over here."

"I don't see anything. Shall we get the cats settled in? Maybe lock them in the bathroom while we eat so they don't get lost and have an accident?"

"Sure—ouch!" The masked kitten leaped out of her arms and ran down the walkway. "Oh, no! Little

Pie, come back!" She thrust the boy at Dylan and raced after the kitten, her long legs flying. That little ball of fluff was moving so fast, she was a blur of black and white.

"Come back, kitty, come back!" Charly's voice trailed behind her. As dusk fell, the rogue feline disappeared into the graveyard followed closely by the most interesting woman he'd met in his life. And given who and what he knew about Cat's Paw Cove, that was saying a *lot*.

The smell of something burning wafted under his nose. "Oh, crap." He pulled out his cell phone. "Yes, I'd like to order a pizza for delivery."

Chapter Six

"Little Pie, come *on* kitty," Charly cooed. The white tip of her tiny tail flicked in the dusk a yard ahead of her sandaled feet. Close enough to see, but not close enough to catch the coy kitty.

This little bundle of fluff sure has cattitude.

Eyes on the prize, she stumbled through a hibiscus hedge—and stopped short.

The kitten twirled around the legs of the woman Charly had seen from afar, audibly purring.

How could something that small make that much noise?

"I'm so sorry to bother you." Charly reached down to pick up Little Pie. Motor still rumbling, the kitten squirmed in her arms. "My little escapee, small, but fast."

Eyes large, the woman took a step forward and croaked, "You can see me?"

"I know, it's getting dark and you are wearing that black dress, but yes, I can see you just fine." Charly paused. Tears glittered in the woman's eyes. "Are you okay? Do you need a ride home?"

Her gaze swept over Charly. "If I only could."

"It's no problem," Freeing one hand from the frisky feline, Charly pointed in the direction of her new home. "I'm just across the street. I'd be happy to take you home."

"That's very kind of you." She dabbed at her eyes with a tissue, the waning light glinting off her wedding band.

Did she lose her husband?

Clutching Little Pie who had become even more wriggly, she said, "I'm Charly Redbird."

"Marjorie Rhodes. Lovely to meet you. I knew a Redbird."

"Why don't we talk about it at my house? See if it's one of my distant relations." She peered into the murk, searching for a streetlight to get her bearings. "We need to get out of here before it gets pitch black."

"Of course," Marjorie made a shooing motion. "You head on home."

Something was not quite right with this lady of the cemetery. Sure, she seemed normal, what with her perfectly coifed brown hair and makeup still intact despite her tears. In her dark dress and classic white pearls, Marjory could have stopped by after any number of events, work, a dinner party, a wedding—a funeral. Charly would have smacked her forehead if she hadn't been afraid she'd lose the critter gnawing at her fingers. Grief-stricken, Marjorie must have stayed after a loved one's funeral and lost track of time.

"I'm so sorry for your loss."

"That's very kind of you, dear." Marjorie glanced back at a tombstone, the name and dates obscured in the gloom. "It's been a while, but like yesterday to me."

So not today, but fresh in her mind. *We all grieve differently.* Still, this was no place for anyone after dark. She could stumble over a root or fall into an open grave.

"I can't leave you here alone—you could get hurt."

A laugh bubbled out of the woman's throat startling Charly.

"I assure you, I'm perfectly safe." Tilting her head and putting a finger to her chin, Marjorie gazed at her with a thoughtful expression. "You're not like the other ones who come here. Everyone else ignores me, acts like I don't even exist."

"Sorry. Occupational hazard. I'm a life coach, so I tend to be a bit bossy." *Except when it comes to the rich and vindictive.* Clutching the kitten who had stopped purring and started meowing at the top of her little lungs. "You're an adult. I have no business telling you what to do." *Step away from the crazy lady.* "Nice meeting you, Marjorie. I'm in the little house with the green awnings if you're ever in the neighborhood."

Astonishment wreathed the older woman's face. "Surely you don't mean the bungalow that looks like a gingerbread house?"

"Yup, that very one." Charly turned. "I'll be going now. Have a nice evening."

Clinging to the yowling miniature bandit, she trudged over the uneven ground of the cemetery avoiding low hanging palm fronds, Spanish moss, and broken headstones. If it hadn't been for this cat now shrieking in her hands, she'd have spent a romantic evening with a hunky guy, learning what muscles lurked beneath that navy blue blazer. Instead, she'd found herself chasing a stray into a spooky resting place for who-knew-what and met a strange woman who wanted to spend the night in a cemetery.

Could this evening get any weirder?

As she crossed the street to her house, a pizza delivery truck pulled away from the curb. Great. She must have burned the pizza, too.

Head down, her eyes glued to the furry wriggle worm in her hands, Charly gasped at the sound of Marjorie's voice. The woman was standing on her doorstep. *How did she get here ahead of me?*

"You're right." She smiled all the way up to her eyes creased. "I need a life coach."

The kitten stopped fidgeting, and the purring motor revved into high gear.

"Sure." *Curiouser and curiouser, as Alice would say.* "Let me get my car keys and tell my friend I'm taking you home." The door behind Marjorie opened.

"No need," she said, stepping through Dylan. "This *is* my home."

A short time later, when the blackness receded, Big D hovered over her, a worried expression on his chiseled features. "There you are." Relief flooded his face. "I barely got to you in time. One more inch and your head would have hit the corner of the front porch. You were out for a few minutes."

Standing behind him with her fist on her hips, Marjorie exhaled a long sigh. "Well, that was a surprise."

Trembling, Charly whispered, "Do you see her?"

His forehead creased. "Her who? Little Pie? She's fine."

A tiny motor revved next to her head.

"No." She pointed at Marjorie. "Right there. Wearing a black dress and pearls."

"What do you expect me to be wearing for my funeral? Red?" Marjorie chuckled. "Silly girl." She began to wander around the room, stroking the walls. She sighed. "There's no place like home."

Big D scanned the sitting area and shook his head. "Maybe you did bump your head. We should get you to the ER."

"She's fine," Marjorie said brushing at her dress. "Damn cat hair."

Charly grasped his wrist. "Don't you hear her?"

"Honey, the only person I hear, is you—and Little Pie purring. Pizza Pie is in the bathroom."

"He called you honey." Marjorie clasped her hands. "Isn't that sweet. My dearly departed husband used to call me that."

Charly closed her eyes, took a deep breath, and counted to ten. *This is a dream. When I open my eyes, that woman will be gone.*

"Hey, don't fall asleep. That's the worst thing for a concussion."

She blinked, and Big D came into focus.

"Good girl. Don't scare me like that." He stroked her hand. "Let me get you some water."

"Glasses are in the cupboard over the sink," Marjorie called. "But he can't hear me, can he? You tell him, dear."

"You're not here," Charly hissed at the older

woman. "You're a figment of my overactive imagination. Spooked by the cemetery. That's it. I'm tired and suggestible."

"Where are the glasses?" Big D called from the galley kitchen.

"Over the sink," Charly said.

Marjorie grinned. "Good girl."

Speaking through gritted teeth, she growled. "Stop that."

"Oh, my dear, don't scowl. It's not becoming. You come from much stronger stock than that." Marjorie pointed at the conch shell. "Tatesta must have given that to you. She was quite proud of it. Looks bigger than the last time I saw it."

"For the love of –"

Big D walked in the room. "Little Pie giving you a hard time?"

"No, not at all." She glared at Marjorie. "Dylan. Sit down. I need you to be honest with me."

He handed her the sweating glass and perched on a love seat. "Shoot."

"Am I losing my mind?" Sipping at the cool water, she longed for a good stiff drink instead. "I see a woman right next to you—and you don't?"

Marjorie's brow creased. "You are trying my patience. I told you *I* need a life coach and you're acting like *you* need a fainting couch. If that's how you work with all your clients, you won't get far."

"That's none of your business," Charly snapped, and Marjorie put her palms up as if surrendering.

She turned back to Big D. "Sorry. Please. Tell me if I'm crazy."

His smile faltered, and he raked his fingers

through his thick black hair.

He wasn't sure where to begin. Did he tell her about the town filled with supernatural talents, the magical cats, or the fact that the moment he met her, he knew she had powers—and she didn't? The retirement home. He'd start there. *No. Too overwhelming.* How could he tell her Grandma Redbird wasn't the sweet little old lady she seemed to be? *Ah. That's it.*

Taking her small hands into his with some trepidation, he sighed with relief at the lack of shuddering shock on contact. A thrill of excitement set off his magic meter—and something else. With those big hazel eyes, her trembling luscious lower lip, and her auburn hair fanned on the throw pillow, she aroused a craving that he hadn't had in several years. One that would only be satisfied if he could drizzle kisses down her long neck and lick the hollow at the top of her collarbone—and continue downward.

Did she have an innie or an outie belly button? Was the triangle between her thighs as red as her hair— and as soft. He shifted in his seat, aware of a growing problem that drove more socially acceptable notions out of his mind and placed her hands on her belly with great care.

"May I ask you a few questions—you can tell me if I'm out of line."

A tear threatened to spill down her cheek, and she sniffed. "Go ahead."

"What made you come to Cat's Paw Cove?" At

the risk of more arousal, he brushed a strand of silky hair away from her cheek and caught the errant trickle. "You never really told me when I asked you at FFRH."

She blew out a long noisy breath, her lush lips vibrating, making him think naughty thoughts. "If you spoke to the woman who drove me out of Chicago, you'd think I was the biggest fraud in history. If you spoke with my mentor's wife, you'd think I was standing up for justice and the American way. In reality, I was ticked off at having one pulled over on me, and I wasn't going to cave in to a bully." Charly recounted the story of the Meadows heiress and how she was blackballed in the Windy City. "Looking back, I should have printed out the damn certificate and given it to her."

"Doing the right thing isn't always easy," he said, daring to pat her arm, bracing himself for the thrill and wanting more. "So, if your business was ruined, how'd you get the money to pay cash for this house?"

A flush crept up her neck to her face, turning her cheeks red. In a whisper, she said, "Playing the ponies."

"Really?" Now *that* was a surprise. He would have never pegged her for a gambler. He considered the Players at the retirement home. Was she under their protection?

She nodded. "I had help from a little old man." Warming up to her task, she described her initial win and subsequent trips back to the track to meet her tiny oracle. "When that guy said Billy had been dead for twenty years, I knew he was drunk." She shook her head. "I'd just seen my friend two weeks before."

"Have you always been close to Grandma Redbird?"

Charly sat up and pulled Little Pie onto her lap, petting her, keeping that motor running.

"She helped raise me and my big brother, Brendan. My dad was an obstetrician, and my mom worked alongside him at Tampa Community Hospital. They worked twelve hour days, couldn't have managed without her. She was like our second mother."

"Has she always collected shells?" He was moving into swamplands but couldn't stop. Not only did he want to see how much Charly knew, but he also had a ravenous curiosity about the old gal. She was more powerful than she pretended to be, he knew that much.

"Oh, yes." She pointed at the conch. "She gave me that one as a house warming present. Told me she'd had it since I was a baby, said it really belonged to me. She's so sweet."

Dylan suspected there was more to it than being "sweet." Grandma Redbird never did anything without a hidden motive. He restrained himself from revealing *that* tidbit.

"Back to your friend, Billy," he probed. "Why do you think he wasn't a ghost?"

"Don't be ridiculous." She frowned. "There's no such thing as ghosts."

"You've never heard or seen things that other people didn't? What about smells—like cigarette smoke? How do you explain that?"

"Pfft. There's a logical explanation for that. Ghosts—if you watch the TV shows—are vaporous, misty. Billy was alive as you are right now, fully three dimensional and dense. I couldn't see through him." She waved her hand as if batting away a gnat. "There is no such thing as ghosts."

Dylan nodded, "Then how do you explain the fact that you've been having a conversation for the last thirty minutes with the very dead previous owner of this house?"

Chapter Seven

"Now we're getting somewhere," Marjorie chortled and clapped her hands. "That boy is a keeper."

"Shut up," Charly yelled. "I can't even hear myself think."

Big D looked hurt.

"Not you." She pointed at Marjorie. "Her. She hasn't stopped talking since she walked in this house—through you, by the way. How do you know who she is?"

"I can't wait to hear this." Marjorie perched on the arm of the sofa. "Give it your best shot, lover boy."

"Where is she?" he asked.

Charly pointed at her feet. "She's saying you should give it your best shot." She left off "lover boy."

"I met Marjorie at FFRH a little over three years ago. She had breast cancer but fought it like a cat."

Marjorie nodded, "So far, so good."

"She was the only regular allowed into FFRH."

"Regular?" That was the same word Agnes had used in Charly's dream. "As opposed to what? Irregular?"

"Like you, she bought this house for cash—earnings from her cottage industry she and her husband had in Middle River, Maryland."

"Don't you go picking on my hubby," Marjorie huffed. "He just did what I asked him to do."

"He was a numbers runner, and she played the horses at the Pimlico race track with the money he picked up." He glanced at the end of the sofa. "Am I missing anything, Marjorie?"

"You're making me sorry I ever told you that story." She folded her arms. "Quite the blabbermouth, your lover boy."

Charly hissed, "Stop that."

Big D paused. "What'd she say?"

"She said go on." *Two can play this game.*

Marjorie slapped her thigh. "Now the cat's out of the bag."

"Her husband—Cecil—had a drinking problem. A bad one. When they moved to Cat's Paw Cove and into this house, he'd get drunk and tear it up."

"I hate this part," Marjorie interjected. "I didn't have a choice. We worked too hard for him to destroy our home."

"She called the cops and told him never to return." Dylan shook his head. "He wandered into the harbor, and his body was never found. After that, she became ill and had to use up all her savings for cancer treatments. She couldn't take care of the house, and her kids weren't interested."

"They never forgave me for not leaving him."

The woman's shoulders sagged. "They didn't understand. I loved him. Still love him. For better or worse, he was my husband. I regret calling the police that night."

Feeling like she was watching a tennis match, Charly's head swiveled between Marjorie and Big D, taking in every crazy word.

"Although Mrs. Rhodes had no magical powers, the administrators had no choice but to let her in."

"Let's say for a red hot second," and Big D *was* hot in a scaring-the-bejeezus-out-of-her-way, on that she agreed with motormouth Marjorie "that I believe any of this, how do you fit in? And what the heck do I have to do with all of this?"

He shrugged. "I'm not much in the magic department—closer to a regular than a magical. I'm more of a talent scout, like a dowsing rod for supernaturals. I knew you had powers the moment I shook your hand."

"So that makes me what? A medium? A ghost whisperer?"

"Yes and no. You're more than that. You see them and interact with spirits like they're alive. But, there's something more. I can't put my finger on it."

"He's good," Marjorie butted in. "He's got you pegged."

She shot a glare at her ghostly guest and turned back to Big D. "Not so fast there, oh seer of my future. Tell me about my grandmother's powers."

He shook his head. "That's not for me to say. You said you were close. It's up to you to find out."

"Okay, fair enough. What about those other people at the retirement home? Who are they really?"

She was trying to suspend her disbelief long enough to let him spin his story. "Are they in some kind of fairytale witness protection program?"

He grinned. "Even supernaturals get old. Doesn't mean they're not magical, but their powers aren't at full blast anymore. Which is why they live at Feline Fine Retirement Home."

"Okay, sure, why not." Mentally rolling her eyes, Charly wished it wasn't the crazy guys that turned her on. For once couldn't she find a *normal* guy to make her want to tear his clothes off and drag him into bed? The wackier, the hotter. Not bad boys, just off the wall, out of their minds, batty. "Give me the who's who and what's what."

Ticking them off on his fingers, Big D ran down the groups. "The Flower Girls, are elderly wood nymphs, past their prime but still protectors of trees and plants. The Puzzlers are Chinese dragons. In addition to talking in riddles and working on puzzles, and they still like to play with the wind and water—which is why they love Cat's Paw Cove. The Decorators are Genies. They're thousands of years old, they enjoy blending in with the old folks at FFRH and the magical community. The Debaters are trolls, like on the Internet. They argue about everything and annoy people a lot. The FFRH Administrators are brownies—sort of like elves but don't *ever* call them that. They will get miffed. They cook, clean, and keep the place running. They also have a wholly owned subsidiary cleaning company—the one that's been responsible for keeping this house squeaky clean."

"They've done a great job," Marjorie agreed. "Especially when you consider their working conditions."

Something niggled at Charly's brain, a dream fragment. "What about the Players? Who or what are they?"

"The Players are the gods, goddesses, and spirits of gambling—and protectors of certain humans like Marjorie—and you."

"Me? I'm not a numbers runner." She gave Marjorie a sidelong glance. "That's illegal."

"So's having inside information on horse races, my holier-than-thou ghost coach," Marjorie shot back. "Riddle me this: why did Agnes faint when I told her I bought this house and named it Furever Home?"

Marjorie raised her hand, "Oh, I know the answer to that!"

"Shout it out for the class, Mrs. Rhodes," Charly said with exasperation. "Make sure the back row can hear you, too."

"Because," Marjorie replied, "my husband tears the place up and makes the brownies clean the house, twice a night, every night."

Charly translated for Dylan.

His lips compressed as if zipped tight with super glue.

"What, no words of wisdom, Big D? Is she telling the truth? Did you knowingly sell me a haunted house?"

"I can explain," Dylan protested. "I thought of all the people in the world, that you with your, shall we say, superpowers, you ought to be able to deal with him."

Her brows knotted and he could have sworn steam came out of her ears.

"You *knew*? And still, you sold it to me?"

He winced. "When you say it that way, it sounds so wrong."

Charly leaped to her feet, and Little Pie ran from the room. Had the temperature risen ten degrees or was that just his humiliation speaking? Her anger pinged into him like a million unclipped kitten nails. He put his hands out to fend off her rage, but instead, what he grabbed was disappointment, sadness, and self-recrimination. She blamed herself. Not him. Herself. That was so wrong. He had to fix this. Before this, she reproached herself enough for three people. This was adding to her indignity exponentially.

"Please," he begged. "Don't blame yourself. Blame me. It's all my fault. I was trying to help—"

Flames practically shot out of her eyes. "Don't you *dare* tell me how I'm feeling."

Oh shit. Not again. The last thing he wanted was to lose her. Maybe she'd understand—

"I'm tired of men telling me what to do and how to feel." Tears welled up in her eyes, and his began to fill, too. "I was hoping you'd be different, that you'd be better than all the other men I've met."

"Charly, I—"

She cut him off with an icy glare, and his heart chilled.

"Get out. Now."

Saddened and silent, Dylan stumbled toward the door. Somehow, he had to make this right. What could he do? Who could he turn to?

One name popped into his head. *Tatesta Redbird.*

Ten minutes later, Dylan pulled up to the curb at Feline Fine Retirement Home and gaped. With all the moving, blinking, singing, dancing, prancing, lighted decorations, the place looked as if it had been converted to a gigantic Christmas shop. This year the Decorators had pulled out all the stops. Glowing with a million watts of lights, the place could probably be seen from the International Space Station. When he climbed out of the car, he regretted not having noise-canceling headphones with him. Ears flattened, the Sherwood cats at the top of the stairs provided confirmation: Santa Claus coming to town or not, the volume *had* to be turned down.

Running up the stairs, he tossed a nod at the guard cats who gave low growls in response.

Find Agnes, then find Tatesta.

Nearly tripping over the tiny woman in the lobby, Dylan shouted over the din, "Agnes, the music is too loud!"

Whirling on him, the administrator shrieked, "You think I don't know that?" She pointed at a woman in gold lame pants and top and a turban. "Tell that to Ms. I Dream of Genie, here. She refuses to change it. Says she can't hear."

Gliding around the lobby on an area rug in graceful swoops, the elderly woman wiggled her fingers and smiled at him. "Big D! Don't you just love this time of year?"

"I like it better when I can hear," he called.

"What's that you say?"

As she ducked and weaved around the now normal sized Christmas tree, he grabbed onto the carpet and hopped on. "Madame Jinniyah," he clung to her waist and yelled into her good ear, "the music is too loud. The neighbors will call the police."

Rug hovering over the desk, the turbaned woman said, "I lost my hearing aids at DME Bingo."

"Did the Players do that to you?"

She nodded, and a tear glistened on her cheek. "They switched the cards on me when I was looking at the prizes."

"Can't you just conjure them back?"

She shook her head. "No. They have them under a curse. I can't find them."

"Drop me off in the dining room," Dylan growled. "I'd like to have a word with them."

He stalked over to the sniggering group of Players—and swept the cards onto the floor. "What kind of bet did you clowns make this time?"

He rounded the table, poking each of them in turn on the shoulder. Not one would make eye contact. "Not enough that you meddle in human lives, you have to pick on old supernaturals now?"

"It was all in good sport," a cherub-faced bald man protested. "We would have given them back to her at the next game."

Dylan slammed his palm on the table. "When? A thousand years from now?"

"Don't go getting your toga in a bunch, Big D." A silver-haired woman with a classic Roman profile sneered. "We can make your life miserable."

"I don't play games of chance, or did you forget that? Not so much as a lottery ticket—or a Bingo game." He flicked at a pile of chips. "I've seen enough lives ruined for your entertainment, thank you very much."

"What exactly do *you* think you can do to us?" Huffed a matron wearing a red and green flamingo bedecked muumuu. "*We're* gods and goddesses."

"How about if Agnes puts your nasty old carcasses out? No more fine dining, no more brownie service, no more weekly Bingo games."

"Pfft. She wouldn't dare," said a smartly dressed man with a full head of thick black hair.

Dylan waved to Agnes, and she trotted to his side. "These are your culprits. They have Madame Jinniyah's hearing aids."

Arms akimbo, Agnes glared at each of them in turn. "You have a choice. Either return them to their rightful owner, or you're evicted."

Moans and groans were followed by a chorus of "You can't do this to us."

"Oh, I most certainly can. Your powers do not extend to me. I answer to the gods of the British Isles, not to you." Shooing at them with her wee hands, she continued. "I will not tolerate bullies in Feline Fine Retirement Home."

"Really now," the Hawaiian clad woman complained, "don't be ridiculous."

Agnes addressed the two Sherwood guard cats who had glided to her side, "Cassi and Cantiaci, would you please escort the Players out?"

Dylan stepped away from the Players to allow the feline enforcers room to do their work. Backs arched and hissing, the mousers marched in a circle, and the dining room table began to bobble and swirl.

"No, no," shrieked the chubby cherub. "I'm sorry, really, I'm sorry."

"Here," the silver-haired woman cried tossing two tiny electronic ear inserts onto the shimmering surface, "Take them. They're bad luck."

Unperturbed, the sentries continued trudging.

"Please, we can't go back there," the well-dressed god begged. "The clothing is atrocious. Nothing but nasty old sheets."

Dylan snatched the hearing aids and handed them up to the happy genie.

"Agnes, what do you think?"

She tilted her head, and the pusses paused their paws. "You will all apologize to your fellow resident."

Like sullen children, each of the four miscreants mumbled their regrets to Madame Jinniyah.

"If you ever pull a stunt like that again, you'll all be hurtling back to where you belong. No more luxury retirement, no more modern conveniences," she glared at the fashionista, "no more Palm Beach resort wear. Do I make myself understood?"

Nodding agreement, the quartet scuffed at the carpet with their designer shoes.

"Good." Agnes turned to Madame Jinniyah. "Would you please turn down the music? I'm sure the police have received multiple noise complaints, and I really don't need the fuss."

The genie clapped her hands, and blessed silence fell.

"Thank you, my dear." She turned to Dylan. "And thank you."

He grinned, "My pleasure. Have you seen Tatesta? I need to speak to her. It's rather urgent."

Agnes pointed. "She's right over there, decorating the tree."

Shells. Why did it always have to be shells?

Chapter Eight

Charly strolled down Whiskers Road and admired the holiday lights festooning the street overhead. She checked out the flyer for the Christmas Gala in Tail's Bookstore window, and then admired a pair of earrings at Cat's Eye Jewelry. At Claws N Coif's salon, a blonde turned an OPEN sign over to CLOSED, reminding her that she needed to find her car and return home to deal with Marjorie. She'd put it off long enough.

What exactly was she supposed to do? She was a life coach—not a ghost coach. Or was she? Back in Chicago if a living client had arrived in her office, the first thing she would have done was interview her and find out what her goals were. Just because Marjorie was dead, didn't mean the woman didn't have goals, did it? *What would Fulburt Traugott do?*

As if conjuring the man who created the world-renowned TIKL institute, Charly heard his voice loud and clear, complete with his German accent. "Vot ist wrong mit you, Charlotte? You must start at the beginnink!"

She stopped dead in her tracks staring at her reflection in the window of the Black Cat Antiquities. *That's it!* She had to get back to basics. What does Marjorie want? Turning on her heel, Charly trotted back to her parking place, anxious to get back to what she did best. She'd always been good at coaching people, whether it was in lacrosse, anger management, life goals—or life transitions. That rich witch Meredith Meadows couldn't take *that* away from her. Pulling into the parking pad next to her bungalow, Charly could hardly wait to get back to work. She strode up her front walk, turned the key, and threw the door open.

The coffee table reared its legs in the air, the TV hung askew on the wall, and stuffing from the sofa cushions blanketed the floor. All the kitchen cabinets stood open, and the vintage dishes and crystal covered every square inch of the black and white floor. She tiptoed carefully over to close the beeping refrigerator and slammed the microwave shut.

Someone had some explaining to do.

Meows emanated from the bathroom. *Little Pie and Pizza Pie!*

She opened the door to a chorus of pathetic mewling.

"You poor babies." She picked them up and held them close. "You guys must have been terrified. Who did this?" She shook her head. "Look at me, now I'm talking to kitties as if they'll answer me."

Was it a burglary? Or was it Marjorie's husband?

Heart in her throat, she raced into her bedroom to see if her jewelry box had been ransacked. Untouched, the case sat in its place on her dresser. She sighed in relief, glanced in the mirror, and jumped.

A gray-haired man sat on her bed with his back to the wall inspecting the conch her grandmother had given to her. Twice the size it had been when she left the house a few hours earlier, the brown and white pattern on the shell now clearly resembled a screaming face.

"Who the hell are you?"

Startled the man jerked back, dropping the shell on the bed—through his lap.

Not again.

"You can see me?"

"Yes," she sighed. "I can see you. Let me guess. Are you Marjorie's husband?"

He smiled. "Yes, I'm Cecil Rhodes. That's amazing? How did you know?"

"She stopped by today. We had a nice chat—about you." She waved one free hand in the air while the other clutched the kittens. "Did you tear my house up?"

His Adam's apple bobbed. "Would you believe me if I said no?"

"No, I would not." She set the kittens down. "Do not touch a hair on these babies."

"I'm offended you would say such a thing," he gasped. "I would never harm anyone, especially a Sherwood cat."

"You didn't have any problem ripping up my couch cushions."

"The brownies will come and fix them." He added with a smug expression, "That's their job."

"Did you ever think they might be tired of cleaning up after you?" She recalled how Agnes fainted when she told her she bought the house. "I think the retirement home administrator might be pretty fed up with your antics."

He shrugged. "It doesn't matter. Nothing matters."

"It matters to me," Charly snatched the conch off the bed. "What did you do to this?"

"Nothing, I swear." He looked baffled. "I was only looking at it. Doesn't that pattern look like a man screaming?"

"I think you're projecting," she retorted, but in truth, it *did* look like that Edvard Munch painting. She set it on the dresser. *Did that thing just wobble?* She shook her head. The bottom was uneven, that was all.

"What did Marjorie say?" Cecil wheedled breaking into her reverie.

Charly turned her attention back to the man—the *dead* man. "Why don't you ask her yourself?"

Panic filled his face. "I couldn't possibly do that."

"Wait. You'd rather destroy the house you shared with her than talk to her? What kind of sense does that make?"

"I don't have to answer your questions." His salt and pepper hair fell across his eyes, and his cheeks grew red. "You'd better not make me angry."

"Or what? You'll throw a temper tantrum and break my dishes?"

He turned his head like an owl and stared at the wall behind the bed.

"Just so you know, that's freaky, but you're not scaring me."

Unscrewing his head, he said, "You don't understand."

Charly righted a kitchen chair—in her

bedroom, of all places!—and withdrew a notebook and pen from her nightstand. "You're right. I don't understand. Tell me what I'm missing."

"Marjorie was the love of my life. And I messed things up," he said in a low voice. "I don't deserve her."

"What happened?" Little Pie and Pizza Pie clawed their way up the bedspread, curled up next to Cecil and began to purr.

"I, um, had a disease."

"What kind?"

"I was an alcoholic," he spat out. "You happy now?"

"It doesn't matter if I'm happy or unhappy." She glanced over her shoulder. "Well, wrecking my house matters. But why did you do it?"

He shrugged. "I don't know. I-I-I get upset and the next thing I know, I'm here, tossing things around. I can't help it."

"Like drinking?"

Head down, he nodded.

"Cecil, I'm going to let you in on a little secret." She blew out a long breath. "I'm a life coach. A good one. I think I can help you. But you must have goals, and you must want to achieve them more than I do."

"I want to stop."

"Stop what? Drinking? You're *dead*. What kind of goal is that?"

He laughed. "No. I want to stop this—" he pointed out the door. "It's almost like drinking. When I was alive, I'd feel bad and get drunk. Or I'd feel happy and I'd get drunk. Or, I'd feel nothing—"

"And you'd get drunk." Charly nodded. "Being angry is addictive. The rage can make you feel powerful—it's like getting high, but on adrenaline and hormones instead of alcohol."

He tilted his head. "I never considered that."

"We can work on that. But we need to come up with your action plan, what you want to do. Cecil, what do you really want out of life—or I guess I should say—death?"

"I want someone to find my body." His pale blue eyes filled with tears. "I want to be back with my wife—if she'll have me."

Dylan stood waiting for Tatesta Redbird to acknowledge him as she hummed a jaunty Christmas tune and wove a strand through the branches of the blue spruce.

She looked up, a mischievous twinkle in her eyes. "I just love these Angel Wings for the holidays, don't you?"

"Lovely as always," he agreed. "You have the nicest shell collection I've ever seen."

"My mother was half Calusa, the Shell Indians. Each one has its own story, its own wisdom—and magic. But you know that." She set the box of decorations on a chair. "Why are you really here?"

He shook his head. "I did what you asked me to do, and now your granddaughter is angry with me."

"One must take risks in life, Big D." Placing her cane over her arm, Tatesta clutched Dylan's hand and drew him to a sitting area. "Buyer's remorse?"

"More like ghost's remorse. She met Marjorie

in the cemetery."

"Really? That was fast."

"You knew?"

She patted his hand. "Yes, dear. The Great Spirit gave me second sight. It's not infallible. Sometimes it's off a bit—" she eyed him "—like with you. I would have sworn you were more magical."

Cheeks blazing, he responded, "I'm just a tuning fork for other people's emotions and a talent scout for supernaturals, nothing more."

"Don't undersell yourself, young man." She smiled, and her warmth and kindness flowed over him. "You have many other good features."

"This isn't about me." He repeated what he'd told Charly at the bungalow. "I told her to come see you, to find out what your powers were. It wasn't my story to tell."

"You're quite right," she nodded. "But it's not mine either."

"What? You're a powerful Calusa medicine woman. How is that not yours?"

She chuckled. "Yes, of course. But she must learn who she is—and she must do it on her own."

"I did sense something more than just her ability to communicate with the dead." He reflected on the jolt he'd received from Charly. "She knocked me off my feet. Said it was static electricity—but it was more like I'd hit an exposed high voltage wire."

Tatesta looked pensive. "Were you near the conch shell?"

"Yes—but how did you know?"

A Cheshire cat grin grew on her face. "Lucky guess."

Lucky guess, my Aunt Fanny. She was up to

something.

"Charly's new to all this stuff. It's not fair to leave her to fend for herself." And leave him as the fall guy and ruin his chances for a relationship with her. "If you'd just talk to her, tell her the truth, maybe she wouldn't be so upset."

"She'll be fine, you'll see. Charly is a smart girl, very resourceful." Tatesta rose and leaned on her cane. "Would you like to come to Bingo with me?"

"I don't gamble, remember?" Was she getting forgetful? "Not a fan."

She jerked him to his feet with surprising strength. "You're coming to Bingo with me."

All conversation in the lobby and sitting area ceased, and heads swiveled in his direction. The Players frowned at Dylan, the Flower Girls clucked their disapproval, the Puzzlers looked displeased—even the Trolls looked more annoyed than usual.

"You see," Tatesta continued. "It's not a request."

She pulled a small conch out of her pocket, raised it to her mouth, and whistled. Windows and doors slammed shut, locks slid into place, and the residents stood in formation.

Ready to do what? Dylan had never feared anyone at FFRH, no matter how powerful—until now.

"I don't understand," he whirled around, still tethered to Tatesta's vise-like grip. "What's going on? Did I do something wrong?"

"No, dear boy," Tatesta soothed. "We're keeping you from hurting yourself—and Charly's future."

Heart jackhammering in his chest, sweat dripping down his back, Dylan's fight, flight or freeze instincts warred with one another. Sure, she's Charly's grandmother—or is she really? Was this really a retirement home for old supernaturals? Or was it a prison for miscreant magicals? Was the head administrator really the warden of a paranormal penal colony? Where was she anyway?

"Agnes!" he called. "Where are you? I need a little help here."

"Big D, please," Tatesta crooned and pulled him toward the Bingo hall. "She's supervising her cleaning brownies. Night is the busiest time for them."

"This is very weird, not like you at all," he pleaded, fear ratcheting his voice up an octave. "You're scaring me."

Laughing, she shook her head and continued to pull him along. "It's just a game, dear. Nothing more. You have anything to bet? Say, a back brace under that blazer?"

Dylan shook his head. *It's a dream. I'm home in bed, sound asleep.*

"Wake up!" he shouted.

And the shuffling supernaturals laughed.

Chapter Nine

Charly tapped her chin with the pen and gazed at Cecil Rhodes. He must have been a looker in his day. With that cleft chin and boyish look, he probably charmed Marjorie right out of her—

"Oh, hello," a squeaking voice broke into her deliberations. "We didn't know anyone was home. We can come back."

Agnes stood in the doorway to the bedroom wearing an apron and clutching a feather duster.

"No, please stay. I'm just having a chat with Mr. Rhodes." She turned to point at him—but he had vanished. "He was just here."

"He's always so embarrassed after he has one of these episodes." The little woman shook her head. "Can't help himself, the poor man."

"You know about him?"

"Oh yes," she said with that hint of a British accent Charly had noticed before. "He's been up to this quite a while—even before Marjorie joined us at

FFRH. We cleaned for her then and saw what he could do. She swore us to secrecy, of course. Poor woman was so mortified. She felt guilty for tossing him out that night." Agnes shrugged. "What choice did she have?"

"How does this work?" Charly asked. "What are your prices for nightly cleaning and restoration—" she waved her hands around "—of this mess?"

Mirth filled the woman's face. "Payment? We don't expect any payment."

"That seems unfair."

"No, no. This is what we *do*. We live for these moments."

Charly chewed on that for a moment. "Do you do this all over Cat's Paw Cove?"

"For those who request our services, yes, but not all do. Some like to take matters in their own hands." Agnes frowned. "Very frustrating at times."

"I understand you clean and put things back where they belong—but the pillows he tore up? Can you really repair them overnight?"

Another tiny person, a man, stuck his head in the door and waved a cushion. "All done."

"This is Harold," Agnes said. "My husband. He does all the repair work, don't you, love?" Smiling, she pinched his cheek, and he blushed. "He's gifted."

I'm about to die from cute overload.

"Thank you."

"Do you want us to continue cleaning for you?"

"How could I say no?"

All she needed now was a handsome prince to join her at her side, and she'd be living in a fairy tale—with supernatural sidekicks, but no talking mice. Was Dylan the frog prince, or was he just a toad. She may have been too harsh. The situation wasn't his fault, was it? What did she expect the guy to do? Post an online ad that said, "Haunted house for sale. Good price"? Thinking of him made butterflies take flight in her stomach, and her heart kicked up a notch. That magnetic pull when he was near her? Did he feel it, too? Yes, he was crazy, but the more time she spent in Cat's Paw Cove, the more she realized crazy was the new normal.

Sighing, she picked up her pen and started writing an action plan for Cecil. As soon as she finished, she was going to write a plan for herself, one that started with apologizing to Dylan. Engrossed in her work, Charly barely noticed the light tapping sound. She glanced up, expecting Agnes or Harold to be standing there, dusters and brooms in their hands. No one was there.

She stood, stretched, and glanced at her clock. Three in the morning? Where had the time gone? Wandering into the kitchen, she marveled at how pristine her home looked now. Everything was in its place, and the sweet little couple had even left some cookies on the table for her with a note.

You were working, so we didn't want to disturb you. Hope you enjoy the snack.

They cleaned and cooked? This was too good to be true.

As she bit into the still warm chocolate chip cookie, a crumb fell, and she bent to retrieve it. *Thirty-second rule? I could probably eat off this floor.* She was considering a glass of milk when the kittens flew into the room hissing and spitting and climbed Charly like a tree.

"Ouch, ouch, ouch! What's going on, you

two?" Bottlebrush tails slapped her face as she tried to extract the needles and pins out of her shoulder. "Babies, you weren't the least bit freaked out when the brownies were here. What is it?"

The tapping grew louder. Where was it coming from? She peeked out the front door. No Marjorie, no Cecil. Just the moon and a salt-tinged breeze. The tapping stopped. She shot the deadbolt. It was late, she was tired, and the cats must have spooked themselves. She would have a word with them about their razor sharp nails in the morning.

After checking the slider on the lanai, she turned off the lights. The bed awaited her, and she fell onto it fully dressed. It had been a hell of a day. As she began to drift off to sleep, the room exploded with the light and sounds of a barrage of fireworks, complete with wailing bottle rockets and shrieking roman candles. The bed shook, and the kittens leaped up, clawing at the air.

Bomb!

Charly screamed and rolled onto the floor, looking for cover. The cats cowered and hissed.

"Babies, I'm so sorry—"

Something grabbed her ankle.

She shook her leg, but the grasp only grew tighter.

Was it the bomber? What was he after? She wasn't going without a fight.

Reaching deeper under her bed, she searched for her favorite home defense weapon: her trusty lacrosse stick. Blind with rage and fear, she rolled over and cursed the intruder, swinging wildly.

"You think you can scare me?" Whack! "I'm best friends with a ghost!" Whack! "One call from me, and all the retired supernaturals will be here to kill you!" Whack!

"STOP!" A man shouted. "Ye made yer point, lass. I give up."

Silence fell. The room stopped quaking. Her heart stuttered and hammered in her chest. More angry than scared, Charly pushed herself up from the floor and confronted her attacker.

Shorter than her, but taller than Agnes and Harold, a man with bright red hair and a jaunty grin stood before her with his hands on his hips.

"Will ye look at ye now. Ye are a fine thing."

This is not a test. De-escalate. Get to safety.

She scanned the room for exits. She'd locked the windows, and *he* blocked the door.

"How'd you get in here?" Mind racing, she didn't wait for his response.

If he doesn't leave, I'll go through him. He's little. I can take him.

"Charly—"

Waving the lacrosse stick in front of her, she screamed, "How do you know my name?"

His eyes strayed, and against her better judgment, she followed the direction of his gaze. The prized gift from her grandmother was gone. Only the jewelry box remained on the dresser covered in a thousand white shards and dust.

"Why did you destroy my conch shell?" Gripping the stick harder, she raised it, ready to strike. "Who the hell are you?"

"I'm sorry, lass." He shook his flaming red head. "I shoulda known ye wouldn't recognize me. Ye were a wee bairn the last time I held ye. Charly girl, I'm yer father."

Dylan grew dizzy as he watched the cage of lettered and numbered ping pong balls spin around for the ten thousandth time. Or was it the millionth? He'd lost count after two-hundred. On stage, the Players, draped in togas and gold leaf crowns looked like an escaped cast of Julius Caesar. The four aging immortals took turns calling out the numbers in various languages and larger-than-life voices to the uproarious laughter.

The Flower Girls tittered among themselves, creating daisy headdresses and floral arrangement between marking their cards. The Puzzlers snorted flames at the Players when they didn't win—which was almost every round. The Debaters argued with each call, stomped onto the stage, and insisted on inspecting each colored sphere.

Three in the morning and all he wanted to do go home and go to bed. Didn't they sleep? Did they never tire of this game—and of each other? He'd rather be sitting in the Highway Department and Motor Vehicles waiting to renew an expired driver's license than be here. What had he done to deserve this? All he'd said was that Tatesta had to tell her granddaughter the truth. The next thing he knew, he was marched into the community room, forced into a chair, given ten bingo cards, daubers, and told to shut up and play. Closing his eyes, he prayed to any listening deity to be released from this game show hell.

Tatesta jabbed Dylan in the ribs with an elbow. "Wake up. You're missing the best part."

He leaned his head back on the chair. "Can I go home now, please?"

"Hilarious, aren't they?"

"Their humor is lost on this mere mortal." He yawned. "Seriously, please let me go. I don't know why you did this, but I'll chalk it up to a senior citizen prank. Just open the doors and release me."

"All in good time, my dear, all in good time."

He glanced back at the two large elderly male genies dressed in matching black harem pants, puffy white shirts, and red turbans. They scowled at him. "Are the costumed genie guards at the door really necessary? Seems a bit of overkill—and they don't look happy."

She laughed and rearranged her daubers and cards. "They love dressing up and looking dangerous. They miss the old days when they could poof into someone's life and make it heaven or hell."

Dylan put his head down on the table and began tapping his forehead in sync with his words. "Let. Me. Out. Let. Me. Out. Let. Me—"

A low rumble shook his table. Jerking his head up in time to see the cage crash to the floor, he stood and searched for a doorway that wasn't locked.

Daubers danced, cards slid sideways in crazy geometric patterns, the Players clung to the red velvet curtains, and the chandeliers jingled like windchimes. The bingo callers and audience fell silent.

"Get up, it's an earthquake," he said, grabbing Tatesta's arm. "We need to get to a safe spot."

Tatesta smiled. "Don't worry, dear. This just means it's time for us to go."

Charly's breath came in short gasps as if she'd run an entire playing field and scored a goal. "You're. Not. My. Father."

The short man shook his head. "Ah, I see yer grandmother hasn't been honest with ye."

"Liar. Get out of my house." She raised the lacrosse stick again. "Move out of my way, or I'll club you to death."

He stepped aside, allowing Charly to squeeze by him. She backed toward the kitchen counter and reached behind for her cell phone. Without removing her gaze from the stranger, she pressed 9-1-1.

"Ye calling the police, are ye?"

She wished her glare would turn into a laser beam and burn him to a tiny red crisp.

A busy signal. She tried again, got another busy signal. What the hell?

"They'll be busy attending to all the earthquake calls." He brushed some white dust off his shoulder and shrugged. "I been in there for donkey's years. Canna be helped."

Sparing a glance at the phone, she punched in her grandmother's phone number. To her relief, that number rang—and went to voicemail. "What is going on?"

"Dinna worry, Charly. I mean ye no harm."

"Says the serial killer right before he drags the girl into a van."

His brows furrowed. "I'm no murderer."

"What's your name," she spat out as she

punched Dylan's number. He may have sold her a haunted house, but that didn't mean he wouldn't help her get rid of this living nut job. "Your real name, no aliases."

A smile creased his freckled face. "Now we're getting somewhere. My name is—

The front door slammed open, and Grandma Redbird strode into the bungalow with Dylan right behind her.

"Thank God you're here." She pointed at the trespasser. "Get him out of my house."

Grandma nodded at Charly and turned to the intruder. "I'd say it was good to see you, Rory, but I'd be lying."

In two long steps, Dylan stood at Charly's side and pulled her into his arms. "You okay?"

She buried her face in his chest and inhaled the scents of smoke and pine. She pulled back. "Have you been at a forest fire?"

"Not exactly," he rolled his eyes. "Long story."

The man called Rory squared off with Grandma. "Ye knew it would only be a matter of time, Tatesta. Ye canna keep me in that shell forever."

She thumped the floor with her cane. Once, twice, three times.

Through the open door, cats swarmed into the little house. Big cats, small cats, black and white cats, spotted cats, mackerel tabby cats masked cats—even Little Pie and Pizza Pie came running to Grandma Redbird. Cats encircled Charly, Grandma, and Dylan, all glowing eyes staring at Rory.

"Ye called in the troops, I see." He put his palms out. "I meant no harm."

"You meant no good," Grandma retorted.

"You're a trickster and a liar. You left my daughter one time too often. When Charly was born and Estame died, I was damned if you were going to disappear again."

Bewildered, Charly said, "Who's Estame?"

In unison, Rory and Grandma said, "Your mother."

Chapter Ten

Dylan was glad he had Charly in his arms when her knees buckled. He lifted her up and placed her on the sofa and turned to the hotly arguing duo. "Not cool, guys, really not cool."

Tatesta waved her cane. A masked brown and white cat leaped up on the sofa, curled around Charly's head, and purred at top volume.

"Ye coulda let me take care of the girl. Dinna need one of yer damn cats. Ye know I can heal anyone."

"Keep your hands to yourself, Rory O'Blarney."

"Still at it with the names, Tatesta? Something wrong with my profession?"

Dylan watched the two like he was at a ping pong match with maniacs.

"As if making shoes was all you did, O'Brogan," Tatesta snorted and pointed at Charly who was beginning to come around. "You made plenty of trouble for my family and left Brendan and Estame behind—until you needed to scratch that itch."

He put his hand on his chest. "I loved yer daughter. Why do you blame me for her death? I tried to save her—"

"You got her pregnant," Tatesta snarled. "That was your fault, no one else's. If it weren't for that, she'd still be alive."

"And ye'd not have a beautiful granddaughter—with yer daughter's powers and mine combined."

Charly shouted, "Shut up. Both of you just shut up." Dylan removed the cat from her head and helped her sit upright. "I'm calling Mom and Dad, and we're getting this all straightened out—right now."

"It's five in the morning, Charly," Tatesta protested. "Too early to bother them."

"Mom and Dad are early risers," she said. "Dylan, give me your phone. Mine has disappeared." He handed it to her, wondering if he was doing the right thing.

A pained expression crossed Tatesta's face. "Don't Charly—"

"Mom, is Dad up?" She took a deep breath. "I need to talk to both of you. Could you get him on speaker, please?"

A groggy male voice came on. "What's up Pumpkin?"

"I'm here with Grandma and a crazy man named Rory O'Brogan who claims he's my father." She glanced at Dylan. "And a friend. Please tell this august group that you are my father and mother and they are out of their minds."

Dead silence filled the air.

"Mom, Dad, are you there? Can you hear me?"

A deep sigh emerged from the phone, along with the sound of crying.

"Ah, Pumpkin, I'm so sorry you found out this way. We should have told you sooner."

Charly's shoulders slumped, and Dylan gripped her free hand.

Tears trickled down her cheeks, and her voice fell to a whisper. "Am I adopted?"

A woman's voice, clogged with emotion, said, "We love you like you're our own child. Both you and your brother. We were going to tell you and Brendan when the time was right—but we were afraid you'd go looking for your real parents—"

"Is my real mother dead?" Charly croaked. "Is this—this— *weirdo* really my father?"

O'Brogan shook his head. "I prefer peculiar to weird but fair enough."

Tatesta spoke loud enough to be heard the next town over. "We need to start from the beginning, Tina and Bernie. We need to tell her everything."

Charly's mouth tasted like twenty miles of dirt road—and betrayal.

Adopted. She was adopted.

Trembling, she handed the phone to Dylan. "I'm afraid I'm going to drop it."

She leaned back into the sofa and pressed the heels of her hands into her wet eyes. A cat curled around her neck and began to purr.

In the distance, her father spoke. "Your Mom

and I worked at Tampa Community Hospital before it merged with Memorial. Your real mother, Estame, was admitted in hard labor and brought directly to me." He sighed. "I delivered you, Charly, and Tina—your Mom—helped me bring you into this world."

His kind voice rolled over her in waves, undulating in time with the cat's purring in a soothing cadence.

"Estame had a pulmonary embolism—by the time we figured out what was going on, she was gone." He paused. "Rory was at your mother's bedside, trying to help her. But no one could help your mother, not even someone with supernatural powers."

Supernatural powers?

Charly stared at O'Brogan. *What is he?*

"Go on, Dad."

"Shortly after your mother passed away, your father disappeared. Your grandmother, Tatesta, showed up at the hospital." Her Dad's voice wavered. "Your Mom and I had been trying to have children for years. Your grandmother was in her sixties, already the main caregiver for your big brother. She was worried about getting old and not being able to keep you."

Grandmother Redbird settled on the chair across from the sofa. "I wasn't a young woman, Charly. Tina and Bernie—your Mom and Dad—couldn't have children. I made them a proposition they couldn't refuse—a package deal. Brendan, you and me."

"We adopted all three of you," her Dad continued. "Never had a moment's regret. Until today. I'm sorry, Pumpkin. We should have told you sooner."

"Is my name really Redbird?"

"Yes. When my grandfather came through Ellis Island, the agents couldn't spell Kardinalvogel—

German for cardinal bird. His name became Redbird. You were born Charlotte O'Brogan. When we adopted your little family, we changed all your names, even your grandmother's."

"To keep the lie in place?" She instantly regretted her snippy tone. On the other hand, how was she supposed to feel? More than a lie, less than a murder, totally deceived.

"No, to keep you safe." Dad paused. "We didn't know where Rory had gone or what kind of mischief he would cause."

The man in question stepped closer to the phone but backed away when the crowd of cats arched their backs and hissed at him.'

"I was with ye all along, Charly. Yer grandmother made sure of that."

Her head spun. Rory was spouting nonsense. "If you were so close by, then why is this the first time I've met you," she shouted, her voice hoarse. "Where the hell have you been?"

A smug expression came over Grandma Redbird's face. "Go ahead. Tell her."

"I've been locked up for over twenty years."

Charly gasped. "In prison?"

"No." He pointed at the dust-covered bedroom. "In that damn conch shell."

Waves of sadness, betrayal, and hurt crashed over Dylan, nearly bringing him to his knees. Charly was gutted. He had to get her somewhere safe, away from these battling beings. Right now, she was all that mattered. Not old wounds, not family secrets, not even truth and justice.

"Charly," he whispered to the ball of pain beside him, "let me take you away from here."

She raised her tear-streaked face up to him. "Where ever I go, I take myself with me."

He nodded. "But you don't need to have those two adding to your pain. You need time to process everything." *Like how did Rory get into a conch shell?*

Her shoulders hitched. "What about the kittens?"

"They'll be fine for a few hours without you. Let's go see Cat's Paw Cove. That's what I do when I need to clear my mind."

"Yes, I'd like that," Charly sniffed, and he handed her a tissue. "Thank you."

"Can you walk, or do you want me to carry you to my car?"

A hint of a smile crept onto her beautiful face, "How romantic."

"Allow me to sweep you off your feet." He leaned over, lifted her off the sofa, and pulled her close to his chest. *Protect her, protect Charly.*

"What do ye think you're doing," Rory sputtered. "Ye canna take my girl."

Tatesta nodded, "Thank you, Dylan. Do get her out of here. It's going to get ugly."

How much uglier could this get? Was Tatesta going to club her son-in-law with her cane? Send in her cat army? Charly didn't need to see or hear any more conflict. She needed peace, quiet, and calm. The best place for that was the waterfront.

He strode out the still-open front door,

clutching his precious cargo.

"Big D," her muffled voice emerged from his torso. "You can put me down. I think you made your point."

"Not until we're at the car," he said. "I don't trust that man."

"Mmmkay."

Dylan set her down beside the passenger door and wiped her face with his handkerchief, an all too familiar gesture from his childhood. "You're going to be fine, Charly Redbird. You just need some breathing space."

She pulled his head down and placed a soft kiss on his lips. "Thank you."

A thrill of pleasure raced from his lips to his toes and all points in between. Her kiss was almost as electric as the jolt he'd received in her living room—was that really just today? It felt like a week ago. How could he have this powerful attraction to someone he'd only met in person a few days ago? Sure, her grandmother had helped get the wheels in motion, making sure Big D was the real estate agent most likely to work with Charly. This was more than a casual fling. This was something bigger. And he really didn't want to screw it up. He pulled away from that searing kiss and took a deep breath.

"The sunrises here are electric," he wanted to add, *Like you,* but didn't.

A short drive later, they parked by the harbor. He went around to her side and opened the door.

"Aren't you gallant!"

"I was afraid you wouldn't get out of the car."

"Take my hand, I think I'm stuck," she laughed. "I'm not good at sports cars. You're so tall—

how did you learn to fold yourself into this toy car?"

"It took practice. I hit my head a lot." The shock waves of hurt radiating from Charly had subsided, but not the deep sense of betrayal. Only time would fix that for her.

Still holding hands, they walked along the shore with Dylan acting as a tour guide. "That ship is a museum. The big names in town—their ancestors washed up here. Along with the Sherwood cats."

"What is it with those cats? They're not normal puddy-tats, are they? I swear Grandma Redbird's cats were talking the night I stayed at her place. Crazy, right?"

He laughed, "This whole town is crazy, in a good way."

The first rays of light began to creep over the horizon, driving shadows away.

She gave him a once-over. "What's your super power, Big D?"

"Ah," she'd caught him off guard. *Unusual.* He straightened his shoulder. "Supernatural talent scout at your service. Not magical, really, mostly regular."

Charly slid her hand out of his and placed it on his cheek. "There's nothing *regular* about you, Big D. If you're not magical, how did you know exactly what I needed back there?"

He shrugged. Most women weren't fans of his other gift. Men, according to his last girlfriend, weren't supposed to cry. That's why she left him, or so she said. Was that the real reason? Or was it because she was angry at the world and pushing everyone away? It didn't matter. She was history. Right now, this amazing person was the only important female in his life. If he didn't share with her now, when could he?

"I'm an Empath." There. He'd finally admitted it to himself and her. "Ready to bolt?"

"Oh, then you can feel everything I feel, is that right?" She pulled herself closer to him, insinuating her arms around his neck in a slow sensual rotation, bumping her hips against his. "What does this feel like?"

Heady waves leaked off Charly, triggering an emotional and physical reaction. "Lust." He slanted his mouth across hers and drank her in, hands roaming her back, finding her sweet behind, and pulling her tighter.

She chuckled, "Is that a banana in your pocket, or are happy to see me?"

"I'm ecstatic to see you, and if we don't stop, we're going to be arrested."

Laughing, she stepped back. "Wow. You were right, that is one hell of a sunrise—" she winked at him, "—and one hell of a banana."

Daybreak at the harbor never ceased to take his breath away. Layers of red, orange and yellow filled the sky like a sherbet parfait, casting out the demons of the past few hours—at least for the moment.

Her stomach growled, and his answered.

"How about breakfast? We have choices—right here we have the Boardwalk Cafe. Then there's Purry's, Sugarland, and Cove Cat Café. They all open early. What are you in the mood for?"

She smirked and walked her fingers up his chest to touch his nose. "I'm in the mood for you." Standing on her tiptoes, she yanked his head down, ran her fingers through his hair, and planted a red hot kiss on his lips.

This time the waves of lust hit him with the force of a body blow. She wanted him *now*, and he wanted her, too. But the timing wasn't right. She was in pain, seeking a quick release. He didn't want a one night stand followed by the walk of shame. He wanted more—much more.

Heart hammering, breath coming in rasps, he pulled away. "Rain check?"

Chapter Eleven

Grateful to Big D for postponing her impetuous offer, Charly rode home with a full stomach in a comfortable silence. An idea popped into her mind, and she couldn't resist asking, "Does a trip to the harbor at sunrise and breakfast on the boardwalk count as a first date?"

"Oh, yes," he answered gravely. "In Cat's Paw Cove, everyone knows everything. The tongues and tails are wagging and planning our wedding as we speak."

She punched him lightly in the arm. "Smooth talker. When you put it that way, we'd better hope that *both* my fathers aren't waiting on my front step, polishing shotguns."

The laugh died in her throat. Both her fathers. For a brief respite, she'd been able to set the family drama on the back burner and enjoy her time with a really nice guy. Now, as they approached her bungalow, a knot of dread formed in her stomach.

Big D reached over and held her hand. "I

know. It's rough. And you're feeling queasy. But I'm here with you, and I get it."

"Chicago was a disaster—I failed, came here to reboot my career. Even got my first client—and then this? There should be a rule that when your career is in the crapper, your family life is not allowed to spin out of control." She sighed. "Can't a ghost coach catch a break?"

He squeezed. "You did not fail. You were the target of a smear campaign. A victim of a vendetta because you refused to be unethical. If anything, you were a success. You can look yourself in the mirror every morning and know you did the right thing. How many people would be able to say that under the circumstances?"

She turned the idea over in her mind. *Am I a loser or a heroine?* "How many other livelihoods has Meredith Meadows destroyed? Do you think she keeps a scoreboard?" Charly could only imagine all the X's chalked up in the woman's kitchen—not marked by her, but by a servant, of course.

"Nah, she's the kind of person who plows through life doing what she pleases." He scrunched up his face. "If I was a betting person—and I'm not—I'd wager her luck is running out, and she's heading not for a stumble, but for a descent into Hades without a return ticket."

"Keep talking, you're getting me all hot and bothered."

"Here we are. Door's closed." He pointed at the bungalow. "No broken windows, no smashed walls. I take those as good signs."

"Agnes and Harold might have zipped over to clean up the place." To go in, or not to go in. That was the question. "Do you think Little Pie and Pizza Pie are okay?"

"Your grandmother wouldn't hurt a hair on their heads, you know that."

"But that guy—" She couldn't bring herself to say *father* "—he wasn't a feline fan."

"My guess is that's because he doesn't understand them. He's a stranger here."

"I think he's strange wherever he goes. Is it just me, or did he look like a leprechaun? That red hair? The accent? That cocky grin, like he owns the world. I can see why someone would lock him up."

Big D rolled his eyes. "Not just anyone. Your grandmother."

"Shut *up*. She's a little dotty, but putting him in a conch shell?" She huffed. "She can barely remember to take a back brace to her bingo game."

"Oh, Charly. I can't *wait* until our second date. I have a lot to share with you." He opened his door. "In the meantime, shall we see if those two are still locked in mortal combat?"

Not waiting for her knight in the little red sports car to save his damsel in distress, Charly extracted herself, almost expecting to hear the pop of a cork. She ran up the sidewalk and ripped a note off the door. "They're at the retirement home. Grandma says we should meet them there."

Big D shuddered.

"Are you okay? Are you getting sick?"

"No," he waved his hand. "Having a flashback. It will pass." He gave her a brilliant smile. "Ready to crawl back into my car?"

"In a minute," she stepped into the house. "I want to check on—" The place was spotless. No white dust, no signs of a struggle. Just gleaming counters, a plate of warm oatmeal cookies, and a note.

Harold was unable to repair the shell. Please forgive us. Agnes

Forgive them? She wanted to hug them. She never wanted to see that conch with the screaming face again. "Little Pie, Pizza Pie, are you okay?" She found the kittens in the bathroom with full bowls of water and dry food and a clean litter pan. Squatting down to pet them, she played with Little Pie's fur—then stopped. "Big D, could you come here for a sec?"

He stuck his head in the door. "They okay?"

"They're fine. Does Little Pie look *different* to you?"

"Hmm. Still black and white, still has a mask—wait," his eyes widened. "Her spots—do they look heart-shaped to you?"

"Phew. Thank you. I thought I was seeing things."

A little girl's voice said, "They're for you and Big D. You make a very cute couple."

Charly retorted, "Who told you about us?"

"We have friends at the harbor," a little boy's voice chimed in. "They saw you kissing."

A hand fell on her shoulder. "Are you having a conversation with the cats?"

Astonished, she looked up at the new man in her life and said, "Yes, I do believe I am. And they think we're a cute couple."

"Welcome to Cat's Paw Cove." He laughed. "I told you tongues and tails would be wagging."

"Let's get to Grandma's place and see what's going on."

Little Pie piped up. "That leprechaun was *not*

happy."

"Here we are." Dylan swerved into a parallel parking place and glanced at the porch. No elderly women in rocking chairs, no cats stretching, yawning, or sleeping, not even the two guard cats, Cassi and Cantiaci sat at their posts. Only the over-the-top Christmas decorations sang, blinked, marched, and danced outside Feline Fine Retirement Home. "Where is everyone?"

"Makes me think of true crime stories," Charly mused. "You know when people flee and the food is still cooking in a pot?"

"Agnes would never leave anything on a stove," Big D said, heading up the stairs, "but a fair comparison. It is creepy."

"Which one of you is the dead bulb?" Harold stood on the front desk repairing a string of Christmas lights. "Ah, there you are. They're waiting on you in the community room.

Of all the rooms in all of the world, why did it have to be the bingo hall from hell?

"Go ahead, Charly," he urged. "I'll wait for you out here."

She clutched his hand. "Please don't make me go alone."

"This is family business—"

"They explicitly asked for the two of you," Harold barked at Dylan.

No longer a game area, the space had been

converted to a courtroom. An aisle ran between two rows of wooden chairs filled with the cats and the residents of FFRH. A jury box on the right contained twelve jurors, with two members from the Debaters group jeering and calling, "Throw the bum out." Tatesta, aka, Grandma Redbird, sat at the prosecutor's table and Agnes sat at the defendant's. A Flower Girl took notes and a large genie in a black uniform, his muscled arms bulging against the fabric, stood against the wall. The witness stand contained none other than Rory O'Brogan—but unlike in a traditional courtroom, he was behind metal bars.

The genie bellowed, "All rise. The Honorable Judge Cayetano is presiding."

The smartly dressed Player with the full head of dark hair entered from his chambers, tugged at the sleeves of his robe, and sat. "Good morning, Bailiff Genie." He looked at the gallery. "You may be seated."

"That's the first time I've heard his name," Dylan whispered to Charly.

Placing a pair of reading glasses on his nose, Judge Cayetano intoned, "Ladies and gentlemen of the jury, this is a criminal case alleging that on the night of May 9, twenty-seven years ago, Rory O'Brogan, Leprechaun, and Healer, failed to save the life of his wife, Estame O'Brogan, after she'd giving birth to their daughter, Charlotte. In addition, he attempted to disappear in the blink of an eye—but Tatesta, a Calusa Medicine woman" he nodded at the prosecutor's table "was able to capture him and trap him in a conch shell."

The Judge turned to O'Brogan. "You've already pleaded not guilty, is that correct?"

"I did nothing wrong," the red-haired, red-face

man retorted. "That witch punished me for no reason."

"Stick to the questions, do not digress." He nodded at the jury. "Have any of you heard or read anything about Mr. Rory O'Brogan. If so, please raise your hand."

All twelve members raised a hand. Some raised two.

"Juror number one, what have you read or heard?"

"Oh, he's a rotter," barked a Debater. "A liar, a scoundrel—"

The judge held his hand up. "That's enough. You'll do."

O'Brogan sputtered. "If these bars weren't iron, I'd come through and grab ye by the throat, ye troll."

"Juror number two?"

A Flower Girl twisted a handkerchief. "He's greedy and hides pots of gold under trees and—"

"Good. Next?"

Juror number three, a Puzzler breathed fire when she spoke. "He's a shoemaker, and a good one—but he'll only make one shoe!"

"Good for the peg-leg pirate trade," Dylan whispered to Charly.

"Who's next?"

One juror after another listed Rory O'Brogan's list of character traits and flaws. "He's cunning and charming." "He's impervious to knives." "He has the strength of a thousand men." "He gets drunk—on cream." "He can read your soul."

"Enough." The judge held his hand up. "We have mortals among us who don't have a lifetime to spend at this trial. You're all accepted as jurors."

"That's not fair," O'Brogan fumed.

"Bailiff, do you have the mustard?"

The genie nodded and held up a large yellow bottle. "Spicy."

"If he gets out of hand again, squirt him."

O'Brogan shrank back into his seat.

"What will that do to him?" Charly whispered to Dylan.

"Burn his skin off."

"Ouch." She cringed and hoped he'd avoid that fate.

"Let's just skip the formal proceedings, shall we?" Judge Cayetano said. "Tatesta, what do you want out of this trial?"

Agnes piped up, "Don't forget me!"

"Okay, okay. Go ahead."

"I want him to stop making messes and to clean up after himself. I don't work for leprechauns."

"Strong words from the little woman," Charly said sotto voce.

"What about you, Tatesta?"

"I want him to be a real father to his daughter and son, to stick around and not teleport himself away when there's trouble." She pointed her cane at O'Brogan. "That's why I never took you up on your three wishes. My only wish was for you to be here when your youngest child came into her powers. If it hadn't been for my shell magic, you'd be doing a jig in Ireland, far away from her."

O'Brogan's shoulders drooped, and his chin hit his chest.

"She's a strong girl, with a stout heart, but she's been through a rough patch. She needs you." Tatesta looked around the courtroom. "She needs all of us. We have no idea what powers she has, being half Calusa medicine woman and half leprechaun."

Judge Cayetano eyed O'Brogan. "What do you have to say for yourself?"

"I'm sorry," tears glistened in his bright blue eyes. "It's all true. I would have whisked myself away if not for Tatesta. And now I see my beautiful Charlotte and my heart breaks. Tall and slender like her mother, but with the map of Ireland on her face. Only an arse or an eejit would have left that wee bairn." He sighed. "I guess I'm both."

"I hereby sentence you to be a good father to your children. You are not permitted to leave Cat's Paw Cove without permission, or we will send a Sherwood cat to find you."

Cassi and Cantiaci, the guard cats, hissed from the front row of seats in the gallery.

"If you do not adhere to these requirements, you will find yourself in a mural in the FFRH Dining Room and be condemned to watch supernaturals eat, drink, and be merry for eternity."

A grimace of horror twisted the leprechaun's face and he gulped. "Not that, please, anything but that."

The judge slammed the gavel down. "Court is now adjourned."

Dylan turned to Charly, "Now the fun begins."

Chapter Twelve

Charly sat in her living room across from Cecil Rhodes and surveyed her home. "No damage tonight. You're making great progress." She glanced at her checklist. "How are you feeling?"

Cecil gripped the arms of the chair. "Anxious. I'm not sure I'm ready to face her."

"Where's your script?" Charly and her unconventional client had reworked the words he would speak to his wife so many times she had memorized them.

He pulled a folded piece of paper out of his pocket. "Got it right here, next to my heart."

"Why don't you read it to me one more time?"

"Okay. Here goes nothing. Ahem. My darling Marjorie," he looked up. "Should I keep darling? Or just say her name?"

"I like darling, it's sweet."

"Ahem. My darling Marjorie. I know I put you through hell when we were alive, and I've made you miserable in death. I wish I could go back in time and make it all up to you. I'd change so many things. But, the past is gone, the future is unknown, and all we have is the present. Right here, right now, I apologize for every rotten thing I ever did to you and our family. I'm sorry the kids stopped talking to you." Tears ran down his cheeks, and he rubbed his nose with his sleeve. "I know it was because you never gave up on me. I don't know what I did to deserve you. You are still a better woman than I was ever a man. Will you allow me to be in the plot next to you in the cemetery, my love? If not, I'll never bother you again, I will leave our old home alone, and stay with my bones in perpetuity."

Marjorie materialized next to Cecil, her eyes bright with unshed tears. "You old fool, that's all I've ever wanted." She threw herself on him, covering his face with kisses. The two merged, shadows with substance dancing before Charly's wondering eyes.

She cleared her throat. "Would you like to get a room?"

The two separated, a flush in Marjorie's face, a grin on Cecil's. Holding hands, the ghost couple separated and squeezed into the chair together.

"No, but we do want to fill that adjoining plot," the woman giggled. "We just need to find his bones."

Charly clapped her hands, and the kittens appeared at her side. "What did you find?"

"The last thing Cecil remembered was getting drunk by the harbor," Pizza said, "so we asked the dock and boat cats if they knew anything."

"Let me tell this part," Little said in her girl's voice. "I got that one-eyed, three-legged cat named Lucky to talk. He wouldn't talk to you."

"You wouldn't have found him if it weren't for me," Pizza argued. "You were too busy chasing seagulls."

"Children, please," Charly interrupted.

Pizza's tail bristled like a bottle brush, but he fell silent.

"Lucky told us he saw a man with Mr. Rhodes description," Little pointed her tail at him, "wander away from the harbor and into the tunnels. Your turn, Pizza."

The boy cat puffed up his chest, "I led a search party underground, and we found a pile of human bones with an empty liquor bottle next to it."

"Thank you." Charly patted her leg, and the kittens sprang into her lap. "Here comes the best part." She leaned forward. "I asked for Sheriff Higgins to help. The DNA—" her voice caught in her throat. "—matches that of the hair Sheriff Higgins kept on file when Cecil went missing after you died."

Crying and laughing, Cecil and Marjorie, fell into each other's arms.

"Together, at last," Marjorie said in a choked voice. "How soon?"

Pride and joy-filled Charly's chest. She never dreamed she'd be so happy to help reunite a ghost couple.

"How's your schedule look for tomorrow?"

Big D stood at Charly's side and gazed down at the fresh mound of dirt. *How could a funeral be such a joyous occasion?* But it was. All of the residents of Feline Fine Retirement Home had come to pay their respects to Cecil and Marjorie. She'd been one of them for the last three years of her life, and her happiness was theirs.

Tatesta placed a ring of cowry shells around both plots. "This ring of protection will last forever."

The Flower Girls planted a red hibiscus between the two headstones. "This will thrive and bloom forever, in good and bad times, just like your marriage."

The Puzzlers breathed into a brazier and placed it in front of the bush. "This eternal flame will send a signal to all that love is eternal."

The Decorators waved their hands, and a wooden bench intertwined with flowers and vines of brass appeared. "This bench will give your friends a place to rest when they visit you."

The Debaters placed a rock on top of each tombstone. "If you ever want an argument, just rap these stones, and we'll be right here."

The Players stepped up and faced the assembled group. "She was under our protection, but the only thing we couldn't control was her gambling on love." Cayetano pointed at Charly. "Thanks to this young woman, Marjorie won the biggest wager of her life—and death." He smiled. "You probably aren't aware of this, but you're one of ours, too. I bet you could do it, and this guy—" he pointed at the cherub-faced Player "—bet you couldn't." He laughed. "Guess who has to polish my shoes for the next one hundred years?"

Charly squeezed Big D's hand and said, "Thanks for the help at the races."

"That was me, dear," the woman in the tropical flowered muumuu chirped. "I had such a good time working with Billy. It was like old times, back when he was alive."

"I'm not sure I'm grateful for being driven out of Chicago by Meredith Meadows." She looked up at Dylan with those warm brown eyes and strong chin and her heart stuttered. "Although Dylan wants to send her a thank you note."

Laughter rippled through the group.

"Charly, me lass." Rory O'Brogan stepped through the crowd, which parted like the Red Sea—in revulsion, she assumed. "Hearing about yer troubles with that woman made me angry. I wasn't allowed to travel to Chicago to make her life miserable, but I was able to make a few phone calls."

Big D leaned down and said to Charly, "Once a trickster, always a trickster."

Rory darted a sharp look at Big D, and a mixture of annoyance at the leprechaun and tenderness for her adorable boyfriend flowed through her.

Big D whispered, "I felt that."

"Good," she smiled. "What are you up to now, Rory?"

"Ye have a smartphone on ye?" The red-haired man folded his arms and smirked. "Ye might want to see some breaking news."

Big D whipped out his cell and tapped the screen. He held it out for Charly to see.

A newscaster announced, "In shocking news today, Meredith Meadows, Chicago heiress, socialite, and billionaire has been indicted for money laundering and fraud in a college admissions scandal that grows larger by the hour. Allegedly, Ms. Meadows spent over half a million dollars to get her daughter into Harvard University. If convicted, Ms. Meadows, who has pleaded not guilty and her daughter, who participated in the scheme, could spend up to forty years in prison—"

Hands shaking, Charly turned to the man who claimed to be her real father. "You did this?"

Rory shook his head. "Nah, I dinna do it. She did it. I just helped the Chicago Police Department find out. Did ye know there are a lot of Irish men and women in blue in the Windy City? They were more than happy to help out one of their own."

"Part of me is thrilled and delighted to see that woman fall—" she looked at Big D "—just like you predicted. Another part of me feels sorry for her daughter. I mean, she was a jerk, but she's so young. I can't believe they'll put her in jail."

"Who says being locked up is such a bad thing?" Rory said. "Maybe a few months will get the lass back on the straight and narrow. Her mother, she's a tough one." He shrugged. "She may need a bit more time."

Breathless, still stunned with the news, Charly choked out, "I don't know what to say."

"How about ye say thank ye, and maybe give yer old dad an opportunity to get to know ye?" He put his palms out in surrender. "I'll be good. I promise. Please?"

Across the way, Cecil and Marjorie, arm in arm, smiling at her from the shadows of the palm trees. Maybe she'd gamble on this new family member. After all, hadn't she taken a chance on becoming a ghost coach?

"You're all witnesses," she pointed at the assembled supernaturals. "On my terms, when I say I want to see you. No popping up when I'm working—or with Dylan." She blushed at the memory of their first night together—and the many after. "Thank you—my other Dad."

    Family secrets.
    Extraordinary abilities.
    Truth, justice, and redemption.
    What more could a ghost coach ask for?

About Sharon Buchbinder

Sharon Buchbinder has been writing fiction since middle school and has the rejection slips to prove it. An RN, she provided health care delivery, became a researcher, association executive, and obtained a PhD in Public Health. She is the author of the Hotel LaBelle Series, the Jinni Hunter Series, and the Obsession Series.

When not attempting to make students and colleagues laugh or writing, she can be found fishing, walking her dogs, herding cats, or breaking bread and laughing with family and friends in Baltimore, MD and Punta Gorda, Florida.

Connect With Sharon Buchbinder

Sharon loves to keep in touch with her readers! Please follow her on the following sites:

Website
https://www.sharonbuchbinder.com/index.html

Instagram
https://www.instagram.com/sharon_buchbinder/

Facebook
https://www.facebook.com/sharon.buchbinder.romanceauthor

Twitter
https://twitter.com/sbuchbinder

Goodreads
https://www.goodreads.com/author/show/4417344.Sharon_Buchbinder

Books by Sharon Buchbinder

<u>Cat's Paw Cove</u>
Charlotte Redbird, Ghost Coach
Meows & Mistletoe: A Holiday Anthology (collection includes *Charlotte Redbird, Ghost Coach*)
Taken by the Imp

<u>Other Books</u>
An Inn Decent Proposal
Kiss of the Silver Wolf
Kiss of the Virgin Queen
Some Other Child
Desire and Deception
Obsession
The Haunting of Hotel LaBelle, Hotel LaBelle Series, Book 1
Legacy of Evil, Hotel LaBelle Series, Book 2
Eye of the Eagle, Hotel LaBelle Series, Book 3

Turn the page for an exciting excerpt from
Taken by the Imp by Sharon Buchbinder

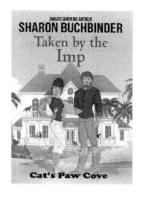

Can a jinni and a warlock cook up a better way to help the poor?

Dexter Graham has no trouble making money as a financial wizard—as long as he doesn't leave his home. He finds it nearly impossible to be with other people, because he's a telepath who gets swamped by their thoughts. Prompted by an unexpected visitor from the past who reveals shocking family secrets, he takes a risk and visits his brother in Cat's Paw Cove. Will the trip make things better or worse?

Ynez Saghira is a gifted chef at the Feline Fine Retirement Home who yearns to be financially independent and open her own café. She has lots of talent and creative ideas but lacks the capital to start her own business. What's a poor imp to do?

Dexter and Ynez join forces to quiet the voices in his head, build her business, and ferret out family mysteries. Will the secrets draw them closer together or push them apart?

Available in eBook and print.

Prologue

Windsor Locks, Connecticut
September

Dexter Graham rattled the cat treat bag and called Brutus for the third time. *Odd.* It wasn't like Brutus to miss a meal. Unlike finicky felines, the fifteen-year-old black Maine Coon cat lived to eat, racing to Dexter if he unwrapped even a cough drop.

His heart kicked up a notch and his stomach roiled. *Something's wrong.*

The sun shone on Dexter's grandmother's well-tended flower and herb garden, which now belonged to him. Butterflies hovered over luxuriant stands of royal red, purple, and yellow. Bees sipped at the open mouths of petunias, ragweed, and clover—the weeds their favorites. A large balm bush, its lush purple color soothing to the eyes, embraced both pollinators. All the little insect people anticipated the cold weather en route, and the garden shimmered with activity in the late September sun.

Still shaking the treats, Dexter sought out the intrepid hunter's favorite napping spot. Not there. *Wait.* Was that—?

"Meow."

"I hear you, Brutus." He circled around the apple tree. No sign of the cat.

"Meow."

The sound was coming from *beneath* him.

Dexter groaned. He loped around to the front of his grandmother's root cellar, leaned forward and pulled on the squeaking wooden door. Sitting on the root cellar's top step, a live mouse dangling from his mouth, the yellow-eyed twenty-five-pound feline blinked and glared at him as if to say, "Took you long enough."

"How did you get in there?"

The cat strutted out. Dexter snapped his fingers, and the cat placed the stunned rodent at his feet.

"Well, it is a lovely gift. I know you worked hard to catch it for me, but I have to tell you, I just ate."

"Mrrp?"

"Thanks for the scare." Dexter bent down and rubbed the cat's ears. *He was safe.* Brutus had not crossed the rainbow bridge to enjoy an all-you-can-eat tuna buffet. "It gets pretty lonely here. Sure, I have Ace, my companion computer, but he's not much company when he's powered down. If anything happened to you, my friend, I'm not sure what I'd do."

"Go to your brother."

"Grandmama?" He couldn't possibly be hearing his grandmother's voice. *It's my imagination. I attended her funeral.* He was in her garden—her favorite place in the world. It always felt like she was just around the next flowering bush, staring off in the distance, having one of her visions. Feeling like a little kid caught with his hand in the cookie jar, Dexter searched for the source of the woman's voice. "It can't be you. You're—"

"Dead?" She chuckled. "That's old news."

"I don't see you?"

"Buckle up, Buttercup—and look up."

A gray-haired woman wearing a brimmed hat, gardening clogs and gloves perched on a large branch of an apple tree. In his early childhood, he'd spent many sunny days roped to the trunk while his grandmother tended to her large backyard. Despite her best efforts to keep him safe while she worked—and had her occasional trance-like visions, he had untied the knots and wandered the surrounding area. He had nibbled at windfalls and created stories starring him as a fearless adventurer. Grandmama's thoughts had broadcasted to him like a megaphone, loud and clear. When she had called, he'd returned home.

"You look good." *Too much time in the sun, that's it. I'm dehydrated. That can cause hallucinations.*

Tilting her head, she said, "Ah, poor baby. You don't think I'm real."

"You're a figment of my imagination. Brutus was missing. I was worried about him." Dexter was familiar with the signs of grief, had worked through them many times. His parents had died when he was four. He hadn't been able to go to school. His brother had moved away. His grandmother had died. And, now, Brutus had scared the crap out of him.

"Dexter." She placed a fist on her hip. "Remember that story, *A Christmas Carol?*"

He nodded.

"Think of me as the Ghost of Christmas Past. Our family made wonderful memories here in this special place. Now, it's time for you to go out in the world and to make new ones. You can't be a reclusive multi-millionaire forever, honey."

"But you—"

"Kept you tucked away, safe from people who wanted to lock you up with a diagnosis of childhood schizophrenia." She shook her head. "As we've discussed before, had I allowed the doctors to treat you back then, you would not be who you are now. You are a brilliant, creative, handsome man with extraordinary abilities, who also happens to be a powerful telepath. It's time for you to leave the nest, get out into the world."

For a figment of his imagination, she was awfully talkative.

"Been there, done that, got the T-shirt, the bumper sticker, and the pins. Remember that disastrous summer abroad trip I took? That was more than enough of the world for me."

"You were sixteen. That was ages ago."

"Not to me." The pain of being led on by a flirtatious college co-ed, only to discover her *real* opinions of him when she'd huddled with her girlfriends, was as fresh today as it had been eleven years ago. "As you know, I tried again when I graduated with my master's degree. A real date, face to face, with a woman I met in my online classes. By the time the evening was over, I was done with her *and* her gold-digging ideas."

"Dexter, not everyone is after your wealth. There are decent women out there—some even have their own money."

"For argument's sake, let's pretend I say yes. Where would I go?"

"Your brother would love to see you. Dylan's girlfriend and I have been chatting for quite a while now. Charlotte thinks it's time for you to visit them. I agree."

He knew Charlotte, his brother's girlfriend, saw ghosts. Did she really see *this* one? Dexter bit his lower lip and mulled over his grandmother's words. Were they, in reality, his thoughts? Personified by his beloved grandparent? "I do owe Dylan a debt—a big one. Fifty-thousand dollars."

"Pfft." She waved her hand. "It's not about the money. It's about family secrets that might shock you—and what the past means to your present and future."

"Why are you telling me this now? Why not before?"

"Don't be sassy." She fixed him with *the look*, the one that had made him freeze as a child. "I was waiting for everyone to be in the right place at the same time. Your brother holds the key. This cannot be done over the Internet. It must be face to face in real time."

"How will I get to Dylan's? I can't take public transportation. The voices—"

"Take Doodle Bug. She'll get you there."

He did have a driving license. He'd studied the driver's manual, and video games had given him the needed practice. When he'd arrived at the DMV, he'd had a moment of panic—until he'd realized the thoughts of the people trapped at the DMV had been a monotonous drone of entreaties to be released from waiting room purgatory. He'd gotten through that day—sweaty-palmed and victorious. With the GPS lady, he could drive to his brother's alone and undistracted by others' thoughts.

His grandmother leaned her head back and looked up into the sky. "Beautiful day. Don't waste it." Like the Cheshire Cat, she faded away, starting with her feet and ending with her smile. "Go see your brother in Cat's Paw Cove. It's a magical place—where *anything* can happen."

Feline Fine Retirement Home
Cat's Paw Cove, Florida
September

Ynez Saghira crushed a few grains of lavender between her fingers and sprinkled them into her test dish: Moroccan lamb infused with the flavors of Persian walnut and pomegranate sauce. More than a few pieces of lavender, and the dish would taste like perfume. Less than that, and it would lose its unique flavor profile. She stirred the red-brown sauce, watched it shimmer and shine, and decided it was ready to be tested. She touched the back of a demitasse spoon to the liquid.

"Madame Jinniyah," Ynez asked, "would you do me the honor of tasting my new sauce?"

Legs folded in a graceful pose, the elderly genie in the red and gold satin turban hovered over the kitchen on her floating carpet. "I was afraid you'd never ask."

Ynez quirked an eyebrow at her adoptive

grandmother. "Since when have you been shy about asking for a sample?"

"Chefs can be tempestuous. Plus, I didn't want to interrupt your creative process." The genie took the proffered spoon, sniffed, raised it to her tongue, and closed her eyes. "Hmmmm." She licked her lips and finally spoke. "Needs more cinnamon."

"Cinnamon? Not pomegranate syrup, walnuts, or lavender?"

"You asked me to taste it, so I'm giving you my honest opinion. I'd like it with a touch more cinnamon."

"You always want more cinnamon, no matter what I make. You have your own shaker at the table." Ynez smiled and took the spoon back. "So, in other words, you like it?"

Madame Jinniyah's hooded smokey eyes, so much like Ynez's own, widened, and she placed a hand on her red silk caftan. "No. I *loved* it."

"Thank you. We'll see what the other residents think when I serve it for dinner tonight." Ynez turned the flame down and covered the pan, to ensure the sauce wouldn't get too diluted from condensate or too dry from the air.

"I think it should be on the menu every night. It could be your signature dish."

"I like that idea. Let's see how the diners review tonight's special first." Stepping to the large sink, Ynez washed her hands and dried them on a nearby towel. "If the Feline Fine Retirement Home residents don't like it, I can always take it to the folks at the homeless shelter in Orlando."

"You spend a lot of time there. Very noble, my darling, but is it what you want to do forever? You're a superb chef. Don't you feel your talent might be, shall we say, *overlooked*, by the diners at that establishment?"

"I love serving them, Grandmother. They're not bad people. They're going through difficult times. I wish I could wiggle my nose and fix their lives." She sighed. "That is truly beyond our boundaries in the human realm. If for one evening a month, I can lift their spirits through food, then I feel I've done something good."

"You are a generous young woman. You make this old jinniyah proud."

"Besides, this dish would be a nice change from meatloaf and mashed potatoes."

"Comfort food for many, my darling," Madame Jinniyah said with a small smile. "Not everyone wants Moroccan flavors like we do. We can't help it. It's in our blood."

Ynez seized on the moment. "Grandmother—"

"Here it comes. You never call me that unless you have a family question."

She dipped her chin and smiled. "You're right."

"What is it, my dear?"

"Who were my parents? What happened to them—really?"

The older woman glided closer to Ynez, reached over, and touched her cheek. "You know the story, darling. Your parents died. I adopted you, gave you your name."

"But we're *magic jinnis*." Ynez threw her hands up. "We're supposed to live for thousands of years. How did they die? A magic spell? A plague of poxes? An enraged ogre? An angry angel? Seriously, I don't get it."

Her grandmother shook her head. "I don't know, my dear. What I do know is you were an infant. You had no parents. I had no children. I begged the Jinni King to allow me to raise you as my own, and he approved. Do you regret having me as your family?"

Vision blurring, Ynez shook her head. "No, not at all. You've been wonderful. I couldn't have asked for a better mother and grandmother. I just...."

"Want to know."

"Yes."

"It's a mystery, my little one. What I do know is you are beautiful, feisty, and you're an imp, a type of genie. Unlike other imps, you are a very *nice* one. You're still growing into your powers. In time, you will see how much you can do."

Ynez glanced at the clock. "What I'd like to do right now is get the rest of dinner ready on time. Can't be caught without our famous fried chicken. Could you give me a hand, please?"

"Of course." Madame Jinniyah nodded, and pots and pans rose in the air, filled with water, and danced to the flaming stove. Vegetables flew onto chopping boards, and knives sliced, diced, and pared. Poultry parts dipped themselves in a seasoned flour, dropped into deep fryers, and sizzled as they cooked. Not a wasted movement between the two, Ynez and her grandmother moved through the choreography of creating the night's dinner for a fussy group of elderly supernaturals, all accomplished without a wisp of smoke.

Read the rest of Dexter and Ynez's story in *Taken by the Imp*, available in eBook and print.

Want more Cat's Paw Cove?
Turn the page for an excerpt from *A Witch in Time* by Catherine Kean and Wynter Daniels

In a violent storm in 1645, Colin Wilshire's Barbados-bound ship is swept off course. He's sure he and his pregnant bride are fated to drown when he's tossed into the sea. He wakes in a strange land and is saved by a blue-haired angel.

Twenty-first-century witch and cat rescuer Luna Halpern has fallen for more than her share of unsuitable guys—including one with a long-distance fiancé, and another who was more interested in other dudes than in Luna. Finally, a safe, drama-free guy is interested in her, and she's confident that she'll muster up an attraction to him. When she stumbles upon a handsome, mysterious man who speaks oddly, seems not to know where he is, or even what century it is, her first instinct is to help him.

Certain he's either stuck in a crazy dream or in limbo between life and death, Colin stays close to Luna. As his feelings for her grow, he's forced to choose between his obligations in the past and his hopes for the future.

Available now in eBook, print, and audio.

Chapter One

*L**una opened her eyes and gazed up at an ominously black sky. Shivering against the damp wind, she tried to get her bearings.*

Where am I?

And why was the ground moving? Not moving exactly, more like rocking. She inhaled and detected the salty smell of the sea. Propping herself up on her elbows, she scanned the surroundings. She was alone on the deck of an old-fashioned ship, like the one they'd raised from the harbor—which had been turned into the Shipwreck Museum.

The floorboards creaked nearby. Then she saw him— a man, leaning on the railing, facing the water. In the darkness, she could only make out his silhouette—a little taller than her brother Leo, and more broad-shouldered. The man's long hair blew around his face and neck, and his loose white shirt billowed in the wind. Gripping the railing, he turned his head her way.

Luna gulped, but knew immediately that he didn't see her. Still, she couldn't stop staring at him. He was...ridiculously handsome.

Only in my dreams....

She studied his strong jaw, chin, and cheekbones. His dark brows knotted. Until his eyes found Luna's, and his gaze trailed down her body, heating her skin as if he'd actually touched her.

Tendrils of desire spread through her.
Ding, ding, ding.

The unwelcome noise yanked her from the dream.

No! She hadn't even gotten to kiss him.
Ding, ding, ding.

She grabbed her phone from the nightstand and shut off the alarm. Squeezing her eyes closed, she tried to return to the ship, to the man.

A rough, wet tongue licked her chin.

"Meow?"

Luna groaned. "You're a poor substitute for my dream guy, Hecate."

The white cat with facial markings like a black mask around the eyes climbed onto Luna's chest and purred. And she knew from experience that Hecate wouldn't leave her alone until Luna fed her.

"Okay, fine." Luna eased Hecate off of her as she sat up in bed. It was almost 4:30, and she had to be at the café in half an hour to start the morning baking.

After pouring food into Hecate's bowl, she stumbled into the shower. Before she left for work, she knocked on the guest room door to wake her brother, who was staying with her after an epic fight with his girlfriend of the month. "Time to get up, Leo."

He grumbled something unintelligible.

"See you at seven," she said. "I fed Hecate. Don't believe her if she acts like she's hungry. And remember, Jordan and I will be leaving the café before nine for the Founders' Day event, so don't be late."

"Mm-hmm," he mumbled.

Founders' Day, ugh! It was going to be a long day, as it always was. But this year, aside from the crowds, period re-enactors, and all the vendors at the park to commemorate the seventeenth-century shipwreck that had led to the founding of Cat's Paw Cove, there was the additional draw of the preliminary opening of the Shipwreck Museum. Luckily, Cove Cat Café was only a ten-minute bike ride from her cottage near the beach—a little less at this time when the streets were virtually deserted. As she pedaled past Wilshire Park, the clock in the tower struck five.

She turned off of Whiskers Road into Calico Court then locked her bike on the rack next to the café door and let herself inside. When she switched on the lights, she glanced through the large window that separated the coffee shop from the cat room. A grey tabby yawned before returning to his nap. None of the other cats stirred.

Luna got right to work, baking enough cookies, pastries and miniature quiches for both the café and their Founders' Day booth. Three and a half hours flew past.

By the time Luna parked the work van behind their booth at Boardwalk Park, most of the other vendors were already set up. Good thing she had Jordan there to help her this year. Luna had a feeling that her very talkative friend and employee would make the day fly past.

The blonde chirped about her boyfriend, Sawyer. "…And he made the most amazing dinner last night." Jordan sighed. "I feel like the luckiest woman on the planet."

"That's great, sweetie." Luna climbed out of the van.

Jordan met her at the back of the vehicle. "My first Founders' Day." She helped Luna transfer cats from small carriers into the large pen at their booth on the boardwalk. "And the fact that it's such a special one—with the opening of the Shipwreck Museum—makes it even better! I'm so excited."

"Mm-hmm." Luna wished that she shared her friend's exuberance for the annual event. She probably should have asked her brother to handle the Cove Cat Café's vendor booth at the celebration, but Luna had always been the one to do it. Besides, she really was looking forward to the time with Jordan. In the short time she'd known the young woman, they'd become close friends. And Jordan's gift of communicating with animals had made the cat adoption part of the café run so much smoother. Hopefully, Jordan's bubbly personality would save Luna from having to engage with everyone who wanted to play with the cats, or hopefully, adopt one or two. Luna's naturally shy nature wasn't suited to working crowded festivals.

Who am I kidding?

The real reason she now hated Founders' Day had nothing to do with the hard work and long hours. But this year she had a plan. This morning she had cast a spell of protection around herself before she'd left the café. Too bad she hadn't thought to do that in years past. She'd have saved herself a whole lot of misery.

"Are you worried about the café?" Jordan asked. "I doubt it'll be busy today. Most of the town will be here. Leo can handle things there."

"I know." Luna had every confidence that her brother would be fine running the place by himself. So why was her stomach tied up in knots? Twice in the past three years, she'd met guys she'd ended up dating at Cat's Paw Cove's biggest yearly event. Both of those relationships had ended badly. But how could she have known that Glen had had a fiancé in New York? He certainly hadn't shared that information with her at any point in the four months he and Luna had dated. Until the woman had shown up at his door sporting a suitcase and a canary diamond.

Then at last year's Founders' Day, Tim had approached the Cove Cat Café's booth and played with every cat in the pen. By the end of the day, he'd convinced Luna to go out with him, against her better judgment. He'd been so handsome and sweet. She should have known that he'd been too good to be true. The jerk had strung her along for three months before admitting that he preferred men. He'd merely been "trying to be straight" for his very-conservative parents.

Yeah, she had a knack for choosing the most unavailable guys. But this year she was safe. She was taken, sort of. As soon as she really gave herself over to the idea of dating Chuck, everything would be fine.

If only she could shake off that witchy premonition that something was going to happen today that would rock her world. No, it was probably just the fact that she hadn't slept enough. She couldn't get that strange dream of being on an old-fashioned ship off her mind. And that insanely hot guy she'd seen there. Must have been because of that news story she'd seen on CPC-TV last night. Several members of the Historical Society had spoken about the restoration of the Guinevere. Luna had paid closer attention because the reporter had interviewed one of Luna's regulars from the café, Roberta Millingham.

The sheriff approached the booth and smiled at Luna. "Good morning," he said. "Hi, Jordan."

"Hey, RJ," Jordan replied.

The sheriff stepped closer and lowered his voice. "I'm speaking to all the vendors before the festival kicks into high gear. I'd like you to let me know if anyone asks a lot of questions about the museum."

"What's going on, RJ?" Luna asked.

His lips flattened to a tight line. "I'm sure you've both heard the rumors that there's a secret treasure hidden somewhere on the ship. And believe me, I'm sure it isn't true. The restoration team has been all over that vessel. Ninety percent of it is completely restored. If there were any treasure to be found, they'd have come across it by now. But, there are still folks out there who think they can find what everyone else has missed."

"We'll call you if we hear or see anything suspicious." Jordan set a basket of cat toys for sale next to the bakery case chock full of Luna's homemade pastries and cookies. "How about a coffee, on the house?" She nudged Luna. "I'm sure my boss is down with that."

Luna grabbed a paper cup. "Absolutely. No sugar, extra cream, right?"

"You know me, Luna. Thanks." Sheriff Higgins grinned. "I hope you've got enough supplies for an army. I heard that ticket sales for today surpassed last year by more than fifty percent."

"Oh, great." Not! As she handed the sheriff his coffee, she glimpsed a crowd of festival-goers, some dressed up as pirates, headed her way. Swallowing, she mentally reinforced the protective shield around herself.

Atlantic Ocean, near St. Augustine, Florida
1645

"They're moving away," the ship's captain said, his spyglass trained on the vessel on the horizon.

Standing on the deck of the Guinevere beside the captain, Colin Wilshire released a sigh of relief, but the sound was snatched by the wind. The gentle sighing of the breeze had increased to an eerie whistling a short while ago when storm clouds had blackened the mid-afternoon sky.

Lightning flashed in the distance, accompanied by peals of thunder that were growing louder. The tempest was headed straight for them.

The storm must have convinced the other vessel—the captain believed it was a pirate ship—to change course.

Still frowning, the captain lowered his spyglass. Glancing over his shoulder, he shouted orders to his crew already working to adjust the sails. Other crewmembers on deck were tying ropes around barrels and nets to secure them.

Fifteen years older than Colin and with graying brown hair, the captain had made the journey from England to Barbados and back again four times. Before leaving the Port of London, he'd gathered all of the passengers together and had warned them of the risk of being attacked by buccaneers. Since families with young children were booked on the sailing, he'd felt an even greater responsibility to deliver the warning.

With Spanish galleons weighed down by riches traveling the waters, and the British also eager to claim a share of the New World's treasures, pirate attacks were a constant threat. The captain had offered to refund passengers' money if they decided they'd rather not make the sea journey, but no one had accepted the offer.

"It's good news, surely, that the pirates turned away?" Colin curled his right hand on the weathered rail and fought to keep his balance as the Guinevere rolled upon strong waves.

The captain shook his head. "Once the tempest is over, the pirates will be back."

"Perhaps their ship will be damaged in the storm. They might no longer be able to attack."

"It's possible." As Colin's hopes lifted a fraction, the captain added grimly, "Unfortunately, the marauders know these waters better than my crew and I. They know the islands and protected coves where they can drop anchor and wait out the storm. They know the reefs that can pierce a ship's hull. They'll let the wind and sea batter us. Then they will come for us."

Crikey. The situation couldn't possibly be so dire. "Can't we also seek shelter at one of those islands or coves?"

"And make it easy for the pirates to entrap us or force us aground? You must not have heard what pirates do to their captives."

Colin had indeed heard some harrowing tales. His cousin, Matthew Wilshire, who'd invested in a small shipping fleet that sailed from London to the Caribbean, had told him the stories after Colin had confided that he was going to leave England. "I wouldn't want anything to happen to you or your lovely wife," Matthew had said, his unusual, pale blue eyes lit with concern. "If I were you, I'd stay in England. I beg you, think about it."

Colin had, over many sleepless nights. Kept awake by his racing mind, he'd sat at the desk in his late father's study and had put quill and ink to parchment—rather ironic, when his sire had always considered Colin's creative pursuits a waste of time. Colin had finished the drawings of his latest invention; sketches he'd intended to show investors. He needed funds to not only make the wheeled contraption, but begin paying off his late father's secret, outstanding gambling debts. Colin had inherited them along with the bankrupt family estate and letters bearing King Charles I's official seal that demanded immediate payment of overdue taxes.

While Matthew had offered to loan Colin some money if he'd stay in the country, Colin couldn't accept. His cousin's finances were already at risk from investing in the fleet. Colin's sense of pride also wouldn't let him become indebted to anyone else, especially a widow with a limited income—his reason for refusing Evelyn's plea to borrow money from her mother. In the end, Colin had decided his only option was to use the savings he'd reserved for his inventions and flee. Perhaps in Barbados, once he and Evelyn were settled, he could look for investors.

In truth, Colin was already a hostage: of his late sire's financial ruin. Could being a prisoner of pirates really be as bad—or worse—than what he'd been facing in England?

As though following Colin's thoughts, the captain's scowl deepened. "The lucky captives of pirates are ransomed. The unlucky ones are sold as slaves or tortured for any bit of information that can be bartered for the buccaneers' gain. And the women...."

Colin thought of Evelyn in their cabin below deck.

"The women are used day and night until the pirates grow bored of them. Then they are sold or slain. Not, I vow, a fate you'd wish upon any of the fairer sex, let alone your wife who is carrying your babe."

"No." Imagining Evelyn facing such horrors made Colin's gut clench. While they hadn't wed for love—their fathers had arranged a marriage between them—he'd known her since they were children, and he cared about her. He had a responsibility to her, and he'd honor it until his dying breath.

If pirates did end up attacking the ship, he'd do all he could to protect her. Guilt grazed his heart, because it was, after all, his fault they were sailing to Barbados. His fault they were on the run and practically penniless. His fault she was lonely and miserable, as she'd reminded him every day since they'd left port.

As the wind rose to a hiss, and the Guinevere tilted hard to the left, Colin struggled to stay upright. Stinging raindrops began to fall from the heavens.

The helmsman, gripping the ship's wheel, shouted down to the captain then motioned to the water.

Colin glanced in the direction the helmsman had pointed, but could see only sea spray and churning waves.

"Go below," the captain said to Colin.

"Tell me how I can help." Colin didn't have much experience with ships, but since the Guinevere had set sail, he'd learned to tie knots, the basics of reading charts, and had fixed a window in the captain's cabin. "I realize you and your crew have sailed in storms before—"

"This is no ordinary storm."

The captain's words echoed Colin's own sense of dread. He'd experienced some strong thunderstorms in his lifetime, watched one recently from the leaded windows of the manor house he knew he was going to have to abandon. Yet, he'd never seen clouds as ominous as the ones overhead.

"Go below," the captain said again. "Stay with your wife."

Colin swiped away rainwater running down his face. "If you need my help—"

"I will call—"

The ship lurched to the left again. Men yelled over the hissing wind, while the soles of Colin's leather boots slipped on the deck and he careened into a post, pain jarring through his shoulder.

He steadied himself, to see the captain staggering toward the helmsman.

A wave crashed over the side of the vessel. Cold water sprayed over Colin, soaking his white linen shirt, and he gasped before grabbing hold of ropes nearby and making his way to the door and the cramped stairway that led to the cabins below.

As the ship groaned like a rusted gate, he stumbled down the hallway to his and Evelyn's room at the far end. Beyond the closed doors he passed, he heard frightened moans, worried voices, and crashes of objects hitting the floor. He'd met the Bells and Harrisons and most of the other passengers, and they were clearly terrified. There were cats on board too; Sherwoods, the captain had called them, a breed that had mask-like markings around their eyes. Two felines were huddled by his and Evelyn's cabin.

Colin thought to knock on the doors and

quickly check on the people inside—the captain and crew needed to focus on the ship, not the passengers—but when he heard a cry from the direction of his cabin, he hurried to see to Evelyn first.

He knocked twice then opened the door. The heat and stuffiness of the dark room hit him, along with a sour smell. Evelyn was clinging to the edge of the bunk, doubled over, her left arm wrapped around her belly. As the ship swayed and the door slammed inward against the cabin wall, she looked up. Tears streamed down her ashen face and onto her gown that even before the storm had badly needed washing.

"Colin—"

She threw up. As he stumbled into the room, following the cats that had darted inside, he saw more vomit on the floorboards. A pang of sympathy ran through him, because she'd already suffered for weeks from severe morning sickness. From the day they'd set sail, she'd been seasick. Being on the storm-ravaged boat must be utter hell for her.

Breathing hard, Evelyn dragged the back of her hand over her mouth. "I...can't stop...."

"It's all right." He managed to shut the door; the cats were now under the bolted-down chest of drawers, where they were welcome to stay. He lurched over to the bunk and on the way, snatched up their spare, clean chamber pot that had been sliding across the floor.

Evelyn squeezed her eyes shut. When she opened them again, tears welled along her bottom lashes. "We're going to die, aren't we?"

"Come now." He handed her the chamber pot, sat beside her, and put his arm around her waist. As he gripped the bunk to try and maintain his balance, he said, "The captain and crew—"

"They can't outwit nature." Her brown eyes blazed as she gestured to her rounded belly. "No one can."

He swallowed hard, wishing she hadn't brought their innocent, unborn babe into the discussion. Neither of them had expected her to get with child so soon after they'd married. It had happened so quickly, she must have conceived on their wedding night. But, a child—any child—was a miracle.

Colin very much looked forward to being a father. He'd vowed to be a far better parent than his own sire had been. Perhaps, if the child were a boy, he'd also be interested in inventing things. Surely Evelyn was excited to be a parent, despite their current predicament.

He stroked Evelyn's hair that was a rich brown color, like polished oak. She'd pinned it up earlier, but now most of her tresses tumbled to her lower back. "I spoke with the captain moments ago," Colin said. "We must trust his experience with storms—"

The ship rocked, and she groaned.

"—and you must trust me," he said.

She glared.

"Trust that I will protect and provide for you, as a responsible husband should." He sincerely meant those words. When Colin had asked about safekeeping important documents on the journey, the captain had told him that the Guinevere's former owner had been a smuggler; there was a secret cavity in the cabin Colin had booked. Colin had brought all of his sketches, protected by layers of canvas and stored inside a watertight wooden tube. After finding the secret spot concealed by crown molding, he'd hidden the tube in it.

Once they reached Barbados, he'd work hard to support Evelyn and not only the child they'd soon have, but any other offspring.

Moaning, she bent over the chamber pot.

He held her hair back from her face until she'd finished vomiting. Then he pulled the linen pillowcase from her pillow and handed it to her to wipe her mouth. He would have offered her water to rinse away the taste of bile, but the pitcher had fallen off the iron-bound trunk they'd used as a table and had shattered.

"I wish we'd never left England." Her words ended on a sob.

"Evelyn, we've talked about this."

"Don't you *dare* tell me to be quiet."

Colin gritted his teeth. "I wasn't going to. But—"

She averted her gaze. Her spine stiffened, and misgiving rippled through him. She was withholding something from him. Something important.

He gently squeezed with the arm around her waist. "What is it?" When she didn't answer, his misgiving deepened. "Are you hurt? Were you injured while you were alone?"

"No," she bit out.

He fought a welling of panic. "The babe. Is it all right?"

"As far as I can tell, it's fine." Tears dripped onto her bodice.

With an eerie creak, the ship listed to the right. She clutched the sloshing chamber pot with white-knuckled hands as he steadied them both.

The vessel finally leveled. The cabin, though, seemed to be growing smaller, closing in on Colin.

Sweat trickled down the back of his neck to blend with the seawater soaking his hair and shirt.

"I was going to wait to tell you," she said.

Bloody hell. He struggled to keep his voice steady. "Tell me what?"

She drew a sharp breath. "It's…it's about—"

A muffled *thud*.

The ship juddered.

As he and Evelyn were thrown several yards across the room, shouts and screams sounded down the hallway. The chamber pot flew from her hands and broke, its contents spreading over the floor.

"What's happened?" Evelyn cried, pushing up on one elbow.

"I don't know." She'd landed on her belly. His heart hammering, Colin struggled over to her. "How are you? Is the babe—?"

"We're all right," Evelyn said.

A muffled *crack*; the sound of splitting wood. Another *thud* that jolted the deck above their heads.

More urgent cries.

"I must go," Colin said.

"No." Wild-eyed, Evelyn caught his hand. "Stay with me. Please."

"I must do my part."

Her fingernails dug into his skin. "You'll abandon *me*? Our *child*?"

"No, I'm going to try and save you and everyone else on the ship. I promise, I'll return as soon as I can…."

Read the rest of Luna and Colin's story in *A Witch in Time*, available now in eBook, print, and audio.

Also Available from Cat's Paw Cove

Artist Samantha Cartwright arrives in Cat's Paw Cove for a visit with her great Aunt Emma, hoping to get clarity about Emma's cryptic prediction. Instead, Sam finds out she must mind her aunt's metaphysical shop while Emma is away on vacation. The temporary job proves impossible for Sam because unlike Emma, Sam possesses no magical powers. Lucky for her, tall, dark, and handsome help enters the shop just in the nick of time.

Eli Kincaid managed to get on the bad side of a ruthless loan shark. Now his life depends upon his ability to con an innocent woman out of the only thing of value she owns—a precious jewel she inherited. If he can get close to Sam, maybe he can figure out where she's keeping the gem. What he hadn't counted on was falling for his mark. Can he escape the web of deception and protect Sam as sinister forces close in on both of them?

Available now in eBook and print.

Also Available from Cat's Paw Cove

Event Planner and earthly Cupid Tori Sutherland enjoys nothing more than playing matchmaker for lonely hearts. Too bad Tori will never find her own happy-ever-after because the only guy she ever loved moved on years ago.

Heath Castillo managed to escape his dysfunctional family for a career in major-league baseball. His only regret was not acting upon his desire for his best friend. When an injury threatens his livelihood, Heath has no choice but to face the ghosts of his past.

When long-buried passions ignite, Heath and Tori consider taking a chance on love. But will the forces that kept them apart in high school destroy their budding romance before it even begins?

Available in eBook and print.

Also Available from Cat's Paw Cove

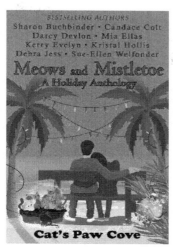

Eight holiday tales set in the magical town of Cat's Paw Cove:

Familiar Blessings by Candace Colt
To repay an old man who brought him out of war's dark shadow, a former Army Ranger delivers a cryptic letter to a gifted medium in Cat's Paw Cove. If what the letter says is true, the reluctant medium and skeptical Ranger must travel back to 1720 to save a young boy from the gallows.

Christmas at Moon Mist Manor by Kerry Evelyn
Lanie and Matt Saunders return to Cat's Paw Cove two years after their first disastrous Christmas there. When a mysterious kitten leads Matt back in time, can he right the wrongs of the past and give his expectant wife the perfect Christmas?

Charlotte Redbird, Ghost Coach by Sharon Buchbinder
With the help of hunky real estate agent, Dylan Graham, life coach Charly Redbird and her new kitten have found the perfect home next to a cemetery. Charly gets a new client right away, who happens to be

her neighbor—and a ghost. What could possibly go wrong?

Gnome For the Holidays by Kristal Hollis
When an empath who's failed at every relationship impulsively kisses an enchanted garden gnome, he magically turns into a real man. Together they must find his one true love and end the curse by Christmas or he'll be forever alone and trapped within his stone prison.

Ring Ma Bell by Debra Jess
In 1979, Michael Bell fell in love with high seas radio technician Dvorah Levi's voice as she guided him to safety, but their marriage was cut short by a bullet. Forty years later, Dvorah still mourns him. Can a special holiday and a magical Sherwood cat bring him back?

Purrfectly Christmas by Mia Ellas
Faerie Sormey Johnson moved to Cat's Paw Cove to live a quiet life as a human until a sexy werewolf deputy needs her help tracking down a murderous monster. When Sormey offers herself as bait, the cost may be more than she bargained for.

Collywobbles For Christmas by Sue-Ellen Welfonder
The fate of star-crossed lovers falls into the magical paws of a time-traveling kitten determined to right an ancient wrong and claim the greatest Christmas gift of all - love.

New Year's Kiss by Darcy Devlon
In order to overcome a family curse, Griffin Brooks, the town's hotshot assistant fire chief, must earn his true love's trust. Trina Lancaster knows she can release Griffin's curse, but will her magical family baggage be a deal breaker?

Available now in eBook and print.

Also Available From Cat's Paw Cove

While clearing out her late mother's home in Cat's Paw Cove, Florida, Molly Hendrickson finds an unusual antique necklace. Wearing it makes her feel confident and sexy—things she hasn't felt since her ex broke off their engagement or, really, ever. She decides to keep the jewel but takes other items to Black Cat Antiquities, the local antique store, to have them appraised.

Lucian Lord, a reincarnated 12th century knight, moved to Cat's Paw Cove after a scandal in which he revealed his magical abilities to his former girlfriend. Demoted by his superiors, he's running the antiques shop while his grandfather is on vacation. But, when Molly brings in artifacts tainted by dark magic, Lucian is duty-bound to find and contain the dangerous energy before it wreaks havoc not only on the town, but the world.

Living by the knightly code of honor, Lucian vows to help Molly, especially when he realizes the necklace is the source of the ancient magic he's hunting. He's determined to save his headstrong damsel and redeem his tarnished reputation—but first, things will get very, very hot.

Available in eBook and print.

Also Available From Cat's Paw Cove

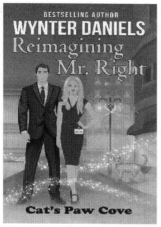

What if Mr. Right was really Mr. Wrong?

Former ugly duckling Sydney McCoy yearns to break into television. And the hottest guy she works with—TV sports personality, Chip Haggerty—could be her ticket to the airwaves. Too bad that Chip hardly knows Sydney is alive. Worse, she has no clue how to speak Chip's sports-oriented language.

Up-and-coming real estate agent Levi Barnett is desperate to convince the owner of a hot downtown property to sell so the company Levi works for can redevelop the site into a multi-million-dollar complex. When he literally crashes into a woman he knew in high school who could champion his cause, he'll do anything to get Sydney's help. All she wants from him in return is help communicating with her office crush. No problem! But when Levi starts to fall for the beautiful Sydney, he wonders if he's making the worst mistake of his life by being her would-be Cyrano de Bergerac.

Available in eBook and print.

Also Available From Cat's Paw Cove

Tired of being hounded by the greedy dead, gifted medium Dr. Theodosia Blessing, the wonder-child of historians around the world, yearned for anonymity. After renouncing her magic, she reinvented herself as Theo, the potter. She returned to her hometown of Cat's Paw Cove, Florida, where she lives with her familiar, a mind-reading tortoiseshell cat named Aloysius.

Former Army Ranger Ethan Cooper was content to live a reclusive life in his cabin in North Carolina. But as Christmas draws near, he agrees to repay a debt to an old man whose wise counsel brought him out of war's dark shadow. Ethan accepts one last mission: to track down Theo.

Ethan appears unannounced on Theo's doorstep with an envelope containing the old man's letter. If what it says is true, the reluctant medium, skeptical Ranger, and wiseacre cat must travel back to 1720 to save a young boy from the gallows.

Available in eBook and print.

Also Available From Cat's Paw Cove

Abby Blessing is cursed. Every time she says the word "love", there's an unexpected power failure. She's tried everything—hypnosis, Reiki, meditation, crystals, vitamins, a Keto diet. Nothing works. Back in Cat's Paw Cove for a short visit, she's resigned to live a secluded life.

Beau Grayson, the sexiest and best electrician in town, is a technical genius with a magical gift to talk to cats. But around beautiful women, he's as tongue-tied as King George VI and has zero ability to manage his office. When an out-of-town chain threatens to force him out, Beau has to step up his game.

With her uncanny organizational skills, Abby agrees to help Beau. But her curse and his inability to solder three words together around her doom any chance for romance.

The only one who believes they are a perfect match is Scarlett, a tortoiseshell cat with a real "Tortitude". Does she have enough kitty magic to bring these two humans together for the happy ever after they deserve?

Available in eBook and print.

Also Available From Cat's Paw Cove

After spending months apart, Matt and Lanie Saunders are delighted to be together again for Christmas. While Matt aided disaster relief efforts across the country, Lanie's dreamed about that white Christmas she wanted for her Southern-born husband. This year, they'll have it all—a Babymoon in Florida and then up to Maine with their families and friends. First stop: Moon Mist Manor in Cat's Paw Cove, where Matt spent many magical summers as a boy.

Lanie doesn't quite grasp what makes the island so spellbinding for Matt, but she knows she'd better not pout. After all, how can she be upset when she has him, a baby on the way, new friends, and an enchanting kitten named Pippi to make her spirit bright?

Just as Lanie makes an eye-opening discovery that puts everything into perspective, she's forced to retreat to the medical suite as a storm rolls through. Matt's outside helping search for runaway Pippi, and it's getting bad out there. Lanie's starting to worry, so Pippi had better scurry if she's going to help Matt make it back for the most wonderful time of the Saunders family's year!

Available in eBook and print.

Also Available From Cat's Paw Cove

Once upon a time, Rachel Saunders told Javier Consuelos she was truly, madly, deeply in love with him. And he ran.

Fifteen years later, Javier still regrets breaking Rachel's heart, but watching her succeed as a corporate attorney confirmed he did the right thing. A long way from his troubled childhood, he's cooking for celebrities and giving back to the community that believed in him.

But Rachel has had a tougher fifteen years than she's let on. When she's offered an opportunity to start over, she realizes her dream job will put her in constant contact with Javier. Distraught, Rachel flees to Moon Mist Manor on Guinevere Island to connect with her long-time feline adviser, Ameerah, who has always steered her in the right direction.

When Javier unexpectedly shows up to make amends this Valentine's Day weekend, and with no vacancies in town, the trio are stuck together. That is, until mischievous visitors threaten to overtake the island. Can Rachel and Javier overcome magical forces and their painful past to save the resort and get a second chance at love?

Available in eBook and print.

Also Available From Cat's Paw Cove

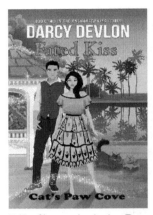

Everyone makes mistakes. Even Fate.

Thirty years ago, one of the three Fates pitted two women against each other, never realizing that the irreversible mistake would result in years of torment for the women's offspring, Raven Lancaster and Lazlo Steele.

Blindly optimistic, Raven uses her gifts as a medium to help others navigate life's challenges. Lazlo, a successful but self-absorbed businessman, chose a darker path, and uses his magic for personal gain. When Lazlo arrives in Cat's Paw Cove, the beautiful Raven calls him out for his inappropriate magic.

At the insistence of his tyrannical father, Lazlo ignores the supernatural community's codes and tries to persuade Raven to let him use her family's enchanted gazebo, which creates a permanent ripple in his and Raven's timeline. When the goddess pays them a visit, she explains that only they can stop this divergence in time. But, is it too late for them to overcome their differences and end the cycle of misfortune?

Available in eBook and print.

Also Available From Cat's Paw Cove

Will past secrets destroy their future?

Former Detective Leda Bellini, AKA Lisa Belmont, has had enough of witness protection. Determined to start a new life on her terms, she shifts into her swan form, ditches her security detail, and heads to Moon Mist manor, a resort island in Cat's Paw Cove, Florida. Somehow, the owner knows her true identity and has been expecting her. Leda is blown away (literally) when she finds herself and a mysterious cat named Davy transported back in time to the year 1717 and into the arms of a pirate with hypnotic emerald eyes. Being trapped in the past may be just the sort of adventure she's been yearning for.

Disgraced Royal Navy Captain Drake Reid misread a command during the Jacobite rebellion that cost him everything. His only shot at redemption is to pose as a pirate and retrieve the magical Avalon roses for the king. Blown off course by a storm, his ship misses St. Augustine where the Spanish are rumored to have brought the priceless treasure. Further complicating the matter is the scandalously underdressed woman who appeared out of nowhere and is now hiding aboard his ship.

Leda finds herself drawn to the enigmatic, Iliad-quoting pirate. On the cusp of achieving his goal, Drake is betrayed, and he and his crew are taken captive. Can Leda recover the Avalon roses before they're executed? Or is their fate already sealed?

Available in eBook and print.

Also Available From Cat's Paw Cove

Three book set! Includes:

Her Homerun Hottie
Will love throw them a curveball?
Event Planner and earthly Cupid Tori Sutherland enjoys nothing more than playing matchmaker for lonely hearts. Too bad Tori will never find her own happy-ever-after because the only guy she ever loved moved on years ago.

Heath Castillo managed to escape his dysfunctional family for a career in major-league baseball. His only regret was not acting upon his desire for his best friend. When an injury threatens his livelihood, Heath has no choice but to face the ghosts of his past.

When long-buried passions ignite, Heath and Tori consider taking a chance on love. But will the forces that kept them apart in high school destroy their budding romance before it even begins?

Gambling on the Artist
Odds are he'll break her heart.

Artist Samantha Cartwright arrives in Cat's Paw Cove for a visit with her great Aunt Emma, hoping to get clarity about Emma's cryptic prediction. Instead, Sam finds out she must mind her aunt's metaphysical shop while Emma is away on vacation. The temporary job proves impossible for Sam because unlike Emma, Sam possesses no magical powers. Lucky for her, tall, dark, and handsome help enters the shop just in the nick of time.

Eli Kincaid managed to get on the bad side of a ruthless loan shark. Now his life depends upon his ability to con an innocent woman out of the only thing of value she owns—a precious jewel she inherited. If he can get close to Sam, maybe he can figure out where she's keeping the gem. What he hadn't counted on was falling for his mark. Can he escape the web of deception and protect Sam as sinister forces close in on both of them?

Reimagining Mr. Right

What if Mr. Right was really Mr. Wrong?

Former ugly duckling Sydney McCoy yearns to break into television. And the hottest guy she works with—TV sports personality, Chip Haggerty—could be her ticket to the airwaves. Too bad that she has no clue how to speak Chip's sports-oriented language.

Up-and-coming real estate agent Levi Barnett is desperate to convince the owner of a hot downtown property to sell so the company Levi works for can redevelop the site. When he literally crashes into a woman he knew in high school who could champion his cause, he'll do anything to get Sydney's help. All she wants from him in return is his assistance in communicating with her office crush. No problem! But when Levi starts to fall for the beautiful Sydney, he wonders if he's making the worst mistake of his life by being her would-be Cyrano de Bergerac.

Available in eBook.

Made in the USA
Middletown, DE
06 February 2025

70292209R00093